A FAKE DATE FOR KATE

CINDY REDDING

A FAKE DATE FOR KATE

Five days before Christmas Kate Thompson boards a flight from LAX on her way to New York for her sister's Christmas Eve engagement party. The only problem she's minus a date and now a prime target for her mother and sister's meddling ways. Not only will she be alone for all the couple activities her sister has planned but Kate's ex husband and his pregnant wife will be there. How could this nightmare ever be merry and bright?

Alex Messina is going to be alone for Christmas. Then Kate takes the last empty seat next to him. On the five-hour flight her talk of an old-fashioned family Christmas, baking cookies, decorating, and shopping has him yearning for the kind of holiday celebrations from his childhood.

She needs a fake date, and he wants a family Christmas. What could go wrong?

For my Family

CHAPTER 1

Kate rushed through the airport terminal weaving through throngs of holiday travelers as she ran to the gate. *I can't miss this flight.* The waiting area was empty. The plane had already boarded.

"Oh, don't close the door. Wait," she shouted, "here's my boarding pass." She waved the paper at the attendant.

The man glanced down at it and said, "You'd better run."

Kate dashed down the jetway, rolling her carry-on behind her. She heard the gate attendant say, "One more on the way." Kate picked up her pace.

A flight attendant stood at the entrance to the plane. She took Kate's boarding pass. "Hurry. Go find a seat, we're full, and the captain needs to pull away from the gate."

"But—"

The attendant pointed to the aisle closest to Kate. "Just go. Hurry up this aisle; there aren't any open seats on the other side."

Kate scanned the seats—three together, four in the middle, and three on the other. She rolled her carry-on behind her and headed up the narrow aisle looking for a seat.

All the passengers were seated and buckled in. Some already had their eyes closed, some scrolling through their phones. A young woman held a baby in her arms; the man next to her holding the baby's bottle.

She was at the back of the plane before she spotted the middle seat between two men in the last row was empty. "Yes, a seat." She almost did a happy dance.

"Go sit and give me your carry-on." The flight attendant startled Kate. In her rush to find a seat she hadn't realized the woman followed her. "All of the overheads are full. I'll store it for you."

Kate turned to the flight attendant. "We're moving?"

"Yes, hurry. Sit. Buckle up."

"Pardon me," Kate said before she had to climb over the long legs of the oh-so-handsome man seated in the aisle seat. "Sorry, pardon me." She may have been rushed, but she wasn't dead. She could always admire a good-looking man. She fell into her seat. Red knit beanie hat on her head. Two bulky sweaters under her caramel-colored Teddy Bear coat, knit gloves in her coat pocket. *I should have found a way to jam the sweaters into my suitcase.*

The equally handsome man in the window seat smiled at her.

"Hi," Kate said to him. "I can't believe I made the flight. L.A. traffic is the worst, and then I couldn't find a long-term parking space. TSA was packed with long, slow-moving lines. I wore most of my heavy clothes. I didn't want to check my bag. Not because of the cost, I didn't want to take a chance on the airline losing my luggage. I can't believe—"

The man turned to her, shaking his head. "No English, no English."

"Pardon?" she said, furrowing her brows.

"*Non parlo inglese.*" He sounded firm in what he said.

Kate looked at him with a mix of surprise and embarrassment if the flush she felt on her cheeks was any indication. It could have been the mad dash through the airport and all of the clothes she had on, but no, it was definitely mortification. Handsome, on her right said something in a language she didn't understand to the man. The other man nodded his head and smiled at Kate, shrugging a shoulder. He took his wireless ear pods from his shirt pocket, gave her another smile, and popped them into his ears.

She sighed.

The pilot came on the intercom with the typical announcements and reminding the passengers that the fasten seatbelt sign was on. Then he said, "We're next in line and will be in the air shortly."

Kate wiggled in the seat. Leaning back, she lifted her bottom enough to work her hand under her, searching for the seatbelt. Naturally, she was sitting on it, and it was buckled. Trying not to poke window seat guy in the ribs, she managed to release the buckle and pull one side of the belt up. *Now for the other half.* She used her other hand to find that side and accidentally brushed her knuckles along his muscular flank. "Sorry," she said. *What good is it? He doesn't understand English.*

The flight attendants were demonstrating the safety features while a recording played. She buckled herself in as the recording ended.

Yes, buckled in. She looked straight ahead and in a hushed voice, she said, "Well, no English, I guess you aren't interested in the fact I *need* a date for the holidays." She shrugged one shoulder and shook her head in resignation. "It's too late now. I haven't been home in two years. I'm going to be dateless—without man—a prime target for my mother."

Kate sat back in her seat and closed her eyes. "I've been on the blind date circuit from hell and to add insult to injury, my little sister is engaged to my ex-husband's brother." She groaned. "I don't want to face my family and friends single again, while my ex-husband brings his new wife to the celebrations. She's pregnant… and she looks like she's twelve."

Kate huffed. "I even wrote a letter to Santa…" She glanced in the direction of the handsome man seated in the aisle seat. "Why am I telling you this? You don't understand English, and your friend is snoring with his ear pods on."

~

THE DROP-DEAD gorgeous hunk on her right shifted toward her and cleared his throat. His baritone voice hummed through Kate. "I never said I don't speak English… I'm American."

She groaned. *Please let this be a bad dream.* Kate swung her head around and stared into the most vibrant emerald-green eyes she'd ever seen. They were set in a face that could easily grace the covers of GQ. High, chiseled cheekbones, lips. *Oh God, yes, he had lips.* His black turtleneck clung to his muscular frame, accentuating broad shoulders, with the sleeves pushed up on his forearms.

"Hi, I'm spill my guts to a stranger, aka, Kate Thompson." She tipped her head to one side. "So, what language were you speaking?"

"Sicilian. I'm Alex Messina." He extended his hand.

A warm, smooth hand enveloped hers. "Nice to meet you, Alex." She gave him her attorney handshake, firm but not muscular, and then released her grip.

"Are you planning to wear your coat and hat all the way to New York?"

She smiled at the amusement in his green eyes. "No, I—" The flight attendant walked by, and Kate lifted her hand. "Miss, can I get two vodkas, no ice and no glass."

Alex leaned over to whisper. "Drowning your sorrows?"

His spicy scent drifted around her; she never wanted to stop smelling him. "No, only my embarrassment."

Alex lifted his dimpled chin in the direction of the non-English-speaking gentleman. "Because he didn't understand you? That's my cousin Matteo."

Kate felt a smile tug at her lips, grateful that Alex was going to ignore her info dump.

Alex said, "I think there's room in the overhead for your coat and hat."

"Great, I'm roasting in all these clothes." Kate unbuckled the seatbelt before she slipped out of her Teddy Bear coat. She pulled her red knit hat off her head by its white pompom, and her hair tumbled down around her shoulders. She slipped one arm through the red sweater sleeve and then her other before lifting the big, bulky sweater over her head. "This is for the ugly sweater contest my family always has."

Alex chuckled. "I hope you don't think I'm rude, but the sweater you're wearing is uglier than the one you took off. This one's neon."

SHE REACHED for the hem of the second sweater and dragged it up before pulling it over her head. "I know. I'm an over-achiever and prepared in case there's more than one contest."

She folded the sweater and as she was about to stand, Alex said, "Allow me to put them in the bin for you."

She raised her eyes to him. "Thanks."

Alex stood, taking both sweaters. *Oh my, he's tall. Broad shoulders and narrow hips, yummy. Stop staring.* She peered up at him through the fringe of her lashes and caught a ghost of a grin on his full, sculpted lips. Alex waited for her to hand him her coat, then he closed the overhead bin. He sat down once again. She inhaled. *I could definitely get used to his spicy scent.*

The attendant returned with her vodkas *and* a glass. "Here you go."

Then she spoke to Alex, "Mr. Messina, we straightened out the seating arrangements for you and Mr. Rizzo. We are bumping the couple who have your seats and will move them back here. The ticket agent should never have given your first-class seats away."

"Actually, it's quite all right. You said they're on their honeymoon?"

"Yes."

"Please let them stay where they are. I'm perfectly content *right* here."

"That's very nice of you," the flight attendant said. "May I offer you complimentary drinks?".

"Scotch on the rocks." Alex turned to Kate. "Would you like another?"

"No, thank you." She leaned into him, lowering her voice. "I haven't opened these yet."

He nodded to Kate and then turned to the flight attendant. "My cousin will probably sleep the whole flight. Should he wake up, I'll let you know if he wants anything."

Once the attendant left, Alex turned to Kate. One dark brow arched, he said, "So... did you really write Santa a letter... asking for a date?"

She'd almost forgotten how she'd blurted that out. "If I were brave, I would have gone to the mall and sat on his lap to ask him."

"I may be able to find Santa's hat, will that do?"

She frowned before she smiled at him. "I know it's silly... I'm thirty-two. I hate hearing all the whispers behind my back. 'Poor, poor Kate, no man in her life. She's always alone.'" She shrugged a shoulder. "The gossip about my biological clock drives me crazy. I'm still young. Anyway, I like my life. I can do whatever the hell I want. I'm really okay with the way things are. It's a little difficult to explain when your baby sister is engaged to your ex-husband's brother. Talk about an awkward situation. I waited until the last possible moment, trying to come up with a way out of this. I thought about asking one of my coworkers to come along as my date… another friend suggested I hire an escort." She rolled her eyes at that.

"It sounds as if all you need is a fake date."

She gazed at him, searched his emerald-green eyes for any signs of pity, and huffed. "You think?"

"You said you're happy in your present situation, and you need someone to be your pretend date for the holidays." He leaned in and said in a jesting tone, "Tell me, do they set you up with everyone and anybody?"

She held the bitterness from her voice. "Constantly. I'm afraid to go home and see who they've dredged up this time. I took the last possible flight so—I'm rambling. I know I've said that already."

"Don't feel like that. I have an Italian grandmother. They're overbearing do-gooders, notorious for meddling. And oh boy, can they lay on the guilt."

"We should compare notes. Like can you top this. FYI, I'm going to win," she said, nodding her head.

He laughed. "I have some pretty good stories, but this time, I'm off the hook—"

"Oh, you're married?" Kate said, unable to keep the disappointment from her voice.

"No." He pointed to his cousin. "They're working on him right now."

"Then you're lucky. I may have mentioned… I haven't been home in two years, since… my divorce, but I couldn't put it off any longer." She let out an audible breath. "My parents are hosting a huge engagement party for the happy couple, along with all the Christmas nightmare activities. You already know about the ugly sweater deal. The ginger-bread house and cookie baking, of course decorating the tree, shopping and… oh, I was warned to wear something formal for the party." She rolled her eyes and huffed. "I want this to be over with. I should have parachuted in for the party and turned around to go home."

His black brows raised. "Parachuted?"

"Yes, you fly in and out on the same day, or overnight if you have to."

Alex nodded. "I see."

Kate continued as an idea began to form. "So, you're willing to help me? My family is umm, very pushy. They'll want every detail and more. I'm not sure I can pull it off."

"We'll be able to do this; I have confidence. Look, I got my grandmother off my back, and that in itself deserves several awards, a Nobel prize of some kind."

She laughed at his jokes and thought he could definitely help her face her family.

He leaned in and lowered his husky voice. "First, can you do me a favor—"

"No sex," she blurted out. *Oh God, why did I say that? Now he's going to think that's what I want. It is but be cool, Kate.*

He crinkled his eyes. "Do you always jump to conclu-sions?" His brilliant smile had her heart racing before he said, "No, not sex. I have to get my cousin on his connecting flight to Rome. Tomorrow, I'm giving a speech to a group of colleagues at the Plaza Hotel. The organization has actually given me a room."

"I'm not going to the Plaza with you." She was sure to sound firm.

"I didn't mean that. You do jump to conclusions. Do you always just assume? I wanted you to know that I have a place to stay, and we can figure out the details later. I'm on that parachute plan as well."

His smile dazzled her. "Why are you doing this? I'm a complete stranger and although you can be a Good Samaritan, I don't think that's it. See, I don't always assume."

"I'm going to be alone for Christmas, and your talk of gingerbread brought back childhood memories. I wouldn't mind helping you out. We'll have to come up with a believable story of how we met."

"Why? Two strangers meeting on a plane won't work?"

He laughed. "No, I don't think so. What do you do? Because nobody would ever believe you would need my services."

Kate frowned at him. "What?"

"I'm a plastic surgeon, and you don't need one thing. What about you?"

"Oh..." She smiled. "Can't help you either. I'm a criminal trial attorney, mostly pro bono. So, if you've committed a felony and can't afford a lawyer, I'm your girl."

"We were set up on a blind date. Does that work?" he asked.

"That's hilarious. My family won't believe it. Even though I've gone on more than I care to say since November... trying to find someone to take home with me. That's when my sister let me know that Brittany, my ex's wife is pregnant."

"Well, smarty pants, what do you have in mind?" he said.

"I'll have to think." She tapped her cheek with her finger. "We have five hours or so to get our story ironed out."

By the time they landed at JFK, Alex and Kate had worked out their plan. She'd go home and the next day, he would give his speech. If she needed rescuing, she'd text help to his phone. If she didn't, and he didn't hear from her then, on Christmas Eve, he'd be her plus one at the engagement party.

"So, we have a plan," Alex said as they walked down the jetway. "You have my number, and I have yours. You know I'll be at the Plaza, and I have your address on Long Island."

Kate couldn't hide her happiness. She had a date and what a hot hunk of a man he was. "Yes, we're set."

Alex glanced at his wristwatch. "I have to rush to get Matteo to his connecting flight to Rome."

She nodded. "Well then, bye for now."

Matteo held Kate's hand. Alex said, "My cousin is trying to say goodbye to you."

She frowned up at Alex. "Oh… okay."

Matteo kissed her hand. "*Arrivederci, Bellissima,*" he said.

Kate smiled. "Very continental. Goodbye to you too. Have a safe flight home."

Alex translated for her, and Matteo smiled at Kate.

"Come on, Casanova. We have to run."

CHAPTER 2

*A*lex watched Kate's cute butt gently swing as she walked from the gate. Her coat and sweaters were slung over her carry-on, and she wheeled the case behind her. All to soon, she was engulfed by the crowd of departing passengers. *She's beautiful and sexy, what a combination.* Alex spoke to his cousin Matteo in Sicilian, "We better hurry to the gate for your connection to Rome."

"She is very pretty. Too bad I don't speak English."

For once, I'm thrilled you don't speak English. "Yes, she is. I'm going to meet her over Christmas here in New York, but she lives in L.A., so I hope to see more of her at home."

"I had a great time clubbing with you and Caroline in L.A. The clubs in Palermo will seem tame after this."

"She does love the nightlife, and now she's filming in Fiji and won't have a break until the new year. Then we're going to celebrate a belated Christmas…What have you decided?"

Matteo huffed. "Do we have time for a drink? I need alcohol before I can tell you my decision."

Alex glanced at his wristwatch. "I think we have time for

a drink. The bar is close to your gate." They found a table and ordered whiskey.

Matteo made a face as if he ate something sour. "I'm going back home and marry that obnoxious woman Grandma picked for me."

Alex laughed. "She's beautiful and comes from royalty—"

"Ha! Royalty that no longer rules; it's just an empty title. She needs me for the money." He gulped his drink.

"Grandma wouldn't have *sold* you into an unhappy marriage."

Matteo spoke more with his hands as he gestured, putting his fingers together. Shaking his hand up and down, he said, "What marriage? I'm telling her first chance I get that we're married in name only."

Alex shook his head. "You may change your mind once you're married. Nothing is ever set in stone."

"We'll see, but for now, they're calling my flight. I have to go."

They stood and walked toward the gate where Matteo's flight had begun boarding. "You and Caroline will come to the wedding once a date is selected?"

"Yes, I won't miss it for the world, to see my cousin saddled… I mean settled down."

They hugged, and Alex left his cousin at the gate. He walked through the busy terminal in the direction of the exit, looking for the limousine driver who would take him to the Plaza Hotel. Alex was honored that his mentor had recommended him to give a speech on pediatric reconstructive surgery.

Alex thought about the woman he'd met on the plane and how cute she looked with her red beanie hat on, and how the white pompom on top bounced and danced on her head as she looked for a seat. He smiled to himself, remembering how she began talking to his cousin. He almost interrupted.

He grinned. Kate's face when he said that he spoke English was one of the cutest things he'd seen in a long time. He noticed her curves when she pulled off the sweaters… She was so bundled up, you would think she were going to Alaska, not New York.

Once her coat and both ugly sweaters came off her clothes were classic. She wore a cream-colored, silk, V-neck blouse that was tucked into straight-leg, caramel-colored pants, a pair of black high-heel ankle boots, and a burgundy cashmere scarf around her neck.

When she said she wrote a letter to Santa, he was intrigued by her and wanted to know more. That had to be a tough situation she was in with her ex-husband's brother engaged to her baby sister. He was willing to help her in whatever she needed. Her beauty was breathtaking; he could see she never had any work done. She certainly didn't need his skills—professional that is—but he would love to show her his skills in bed. He smiled, thinking of her body. He almost missed the sign with his name on it.

"I'm Alexander Messina," he said to the limousine driver and handed the man his bag.

"The car's right out front, sir." Alex got into the backseat. The driver pulled into traffic and said they should be at the hotel soon.

Alex hoped that Kate would call him before Christmas Eve, when he agreed to be her plus one. She'd said it was a black-tie event, so he would order a tux from the men's shop at the hotel. His Gucci, Prada, and Armani tuxes were home in his Bel Air master bedroom's walk-in closet.

CHAPTER 3

After Kate said goodbye to Alex and Matteo, she took her phone off airplane mode and found a text from her dad. He'd parked in the short-term parking garage rather than waiting in the cell phone lot. Once she reached the exit, Kate put on her coat and hat but carried the two sweaters over her arm, and pulled her carry-on behind her. JFK was always crowded and busy, but at eight p.m., five days before Christmas, it was horrendous. Car horns blared as some pedestrians tried to cross against the traffic. Whistles blew as traffic enforcement officers directed cars, buses, and taxis through the lanes. Kate stayed in the pedestrian lane and crossed the street to the parking garage. She saw her father standing on the side and waved to him.

"Dad." She hugged him. Bill Riley was just under six feet with reddish hair and blue eyes. He wore a heavy winter jacket, jeans, and loafers.

"Hello, princess. How was the flight?"

"Uneventful." She ignored the twinge of guilt. That small untruth was nothing compared to what she planned with the darkly handsome stranger she met on the plane. His deep voice echoed in her brain. She and her father walked into the parking garage.

"I forgot how cold it could get at night." She huddled into her coat as they walked to the car.

"I'm going to warn you, Kate. Your mom has a slew of activities planned, and she…well, I'll let you be surprised." They drove home in her dad's old Volvo. It was the end of rush hour, so the traffic moved along, and they made good time to Nassau County.

Kate thought, nothing had changed. The lawn leading up to the house had an animated Santa in his sleigh. On the other side, a snowman lawn decoration stood with his arms full of Christmas presents.

The house, a large white colonial with black shutters, was decorated for Christmas. A wreath hung from a red ribbon on each window. In the center of the wreath was a flameless, flickering candle. Knowing her mother, they were on a timer. Another large wreath hung from the front door, reminding Kate of a scene from a Christmas card.

Her mom and sister Olivia met her at the door. Kate hadn't stepped foot into the foyer when they started. Could she get through four days before Alex arrived?

"It's late, but I saved you some dinner. Are you hungry?" her mother asked.

"Not a big dinner. Maybe just one of your special grilled cheese sandwiches." She smiled at her mom.

"Ben wanted to drop by, but he got stuck at the office. He's finishing up so he can be off for the rest of the week," Olivia said as she sat at the farm-style kitchen table.

Ben, her ex-brother-in-law, soon to be her brother-in-law once more. *How do you explain that without a chart? Apparently, everyone but me thinks it's hilarious.*

"We won't be doing any couple activities until tomorrow,"

Olivia continued. "I'm spending the night, so we can get started early."

"Will I have time to unpack and take a shower?" Kate snarked.

"Of course, we aren't rushing you and… then… maybe—"

"Olivia," Kate's mom interrupted, "tomorrow is soon enough to fill your sister in on all the couples activities."

Her dad came into the kitchen. "I put your bag in your room, honey."

"Thanks, Dad." Kate tried to relax. She was happy to be with her parents. Her mom made grilled cheese sandwiches for all of them.

Then Olivia said, "I'm going up to my room. I want to call Ben." She kissed Kate good night. Kate helped her mother load the dishwasher. Then she went to her room. It was the same as it was the day she left it to marry Dan four years ago. *Except for the Christmas tree in the corner and the decorations.* It was a cozy bedroom with a queen-size bed and its own en suite with a shower. She unpacked, hanging her clothes in the closet. She put her lingerie in her dresser drawer, took a quick shower, and hopped into bed, pulling the Christmas comforter over her. Her thoughts drifted to Alex, the handsome stranger she met on the plane. *What's he doing now? Is he thinking of me?* She tossed and turned, dreading the next four days.

The next morning, Kate and her mom sat at the farm-style table in the large gourmet kitchen at the back of the house. In one corner, her mom had decorated a medium-size live Christmas tree. Popcorn garland encircled the tree and different-shape cookie cutters, small rolling pins and even miniature muffin pans hung from the branches. Morning sunlight streamed through the three large bay windows.

The kitchen opened to the family room where a fire blazed, its flickering flames glowing like a mirror on the polished hardwood floor. In the family room, a live tree decorated in red and green bows, along with different Santas were near the fireplace. All the trees were beautiful, but Kate loved the photos. The mantel above the fireplace was full of pictures of Santa visits. All in Christmas frames, Kate's first Christmas and Olivia's first Christmas, all the way through the years with her and Olivia. Her mom dated the backs of each photo. The nostalgia always got to Kate. Each year, they went to Macy's on 34th street to visit the *real* Santa as Olivia used to say. Their parents would take them to the Thanksgiving Day parade and they would watch as Santa came to town. Then before Christmas, they would go to see him at Macy's.

The main tree in the formal living room would be decorated by all of them before paella night.

This morning, her mom had made her favorite breakfast —waffles and scrambled eggs. Kate hadn't put the first bite of her scrambled egg in her mouth when her mom began.

"We have so many fun activities planned. I know you didn't have time to get a date, so your sister and I put our heads together and made a list of all your old friends to see who was single and available. Remember that nice Chris Jones from—"

"From kindergarten, Mom. You had to go back that far?" Kate slipped her iPhone from her pocket and held it on her lap under the table.

HELP. She smiled up at her mom, keeping her phone under the table as she pressed send.

"Can I borrow the car? I have to go pick up Alex."

"Alex, who is he?"

"He's... my date. He couldn't come on the same flight I did. I'm going to pick him up at... the... airport. He can stay in the guest bedroom."

Her sister practically skipped into the kitchen, "Good

morning. I'm so happy you're here." She hugged Kate. "Did you tell her?" Olivia's voice bubbled with cheer.

Kate kept her voice calm. "As a matter of fact, Mom did, but I have my own date. Thanks just the same."

"Really, I wish we'd known. We wouldn't have had to look for someone for you. I'll have to call Chris right now, so he doesn't come over tonight. You know we're all going to dinner at that nice restaurant at the inn. You know the one on the water. You'll get to meet Daniel's wife Brittany. I can't believe that your ex-husband is going to be my brother-in-law again." Olivia covered her mouth, hiding a giggle. "We joked about that when Ben and I began dating."

Kate kept her comments to herself, not wanting her family to know how awkward she thought the whole situation was. Was she the only one who remembered how her husband Dan dragged her to L.A., away from her family? How once she settled into her job at the law firm, he cheated on her with Brittany, and how Dan told her he was moving back to New York with his new love... the same Brittany Olivia wants her to meet.

Her phone vibrated, startling her. She glanced down at the screen.

Meet me now. You can join me for lunch, and then I will give my speech. We can be out and on our way by two thirty to three at the latest.

She texted back. **Okay, the Plaza hotel, correct?**

Yes, I'll leave your name at the front desk, and you can meet me in the Palm Court Restaurant, where the conference is being held.

She glanced up at her mother. "So, can I borrow the car?"

"Yes, of course you can. I'll come with you."

"No, I want to go alone. You'll meet him soon enough."

"When did you meet him?" Olivia asked

"What does he do?" her mom asked.

"How long have you been seeing him?" Olivia asked.

They bombarded her with questions. *On the plane yesterday.* "I met him… in… October. He's a doctor. Actually, a plastic surgeon. We've been dating since… we met. I have to change before I go."

Kate hurried out of the kitchen before either her mother or sister had a chance to ask her further questions. She ran up the steps and into her room. She hadn't brought too many clothes and chose outfits that coordinated with each other. She picked up the body-hugging cream-colored sweater dress she brought along. She buckled a black leather belt around her waist. She put on her designer gold teardrop earrings and her gold bangle bracelet. She stepped into the black ankle boots from yesterday. Smoothed her hair, checked her makeup, and hurried out of the house.

CHAPTER 4

*A*lex was thrilled when Kate texted him. He wanted to see her sexy body before her sister's engagement party on Christmas Eve. From what she told him, her ex-husband had been a bastard, and Alex wanted to help her save face from the embarrassment of attending without a date. When she told him about the gingerbread house contest and some other traditions, it reminded him of Christmas with his parents and younger sister Caroline. He missed those days.

Her text worked out perfectly. Kate would meet him in the Palm Court Restaurant of the Plaza Hotel. The entire room was reserved for this event. A piano subtly played Christmas songs. Alex glanced toward the entrance, looking for Kate. When she walked into the room, she broke out into a huge smile and waved to him. He excused himself from an associate and walked over to her.

"Hello Kate. You look beautiful."

"Hi, I made pretty good time getting here. Thanks for agreeing to meet me earlier than we planned," Kate said.

"You have a seat next to me on the dais, along with the

other speaker and his wife." He put his hand on the small of her back as he led her to their seats. Her scent of wildflowers drifted around him. "I ordered the filet for both of us. I hope that's good."

"Yes, that's great." She smiled up at him.

"We're about to start. I hope you don't find the speeches boring," he said as he held her seat for her.

They talked through lunch, and Alex found her to be delightful and funny.

"My mother and sister hadn't given me a chance to walk in the door last night when I was bombarded with all the plans. You had to see their faces when I said I had a date." Kate laughed.

"We will be sure to lay it on thick for them."

"This will be fun. I can't wait."

Alex said, "I have to change and get my bag. Would you like to wait in the lounge?" He didn't want her to feel uncomfortable after her remarks yesterday. Alex changed out of his suit and tie before he met Kate in the lobby. He wore faded denim jeans and a crewneck sweater, with a white shirt under. He carried his coat on his arm, and his designer garment bag was slung over his shoulder. "Ready for the fake-out?"

"I hope I can pull this off with you," she said, touching his arm.

"Why not?"

"My mom had a slew of questions, but I did what you suggested and gave as much truth as possible. There are no grey areas in my life, so I was a little nervous. Be prepared for the third degree from both my mom and sister."

"I'm ready for their questions."

Once they were in the car, Kate said, "I was very impressed by your speech on pediatric reconstructive surgery. And here I thought you had a lucrative practice in Beverly Hills doing boob jobs and tummy tucks."

He laughed before he said, "Boob jobs and tummy tucks, yes, I do those. Helping young children is a passion of mine."

"We're almost to my parents' home. I want to prepare you. My sister Olivia is clueless over how uncomfortable this situation is for me. She even thinks Britany and I will become friends. She has all these couples activities planned. All merry and bright, but I feel–what's the opposite of merry?"

"Don't concern yourself. I'm going to make your ex regret leaving you and help you forget his name."

"That's a tall order. I mean his regret, but honestly I've moved on. It certainly would have been better if I never had to see him again."

Kate parked the car in the driveway and brought Alex into the house from the main entrance into the foyer. "Leave your bag here temporarily and give me your coat." She hung up both their coats in the hall closet. "Hello, we're here," she said as she led Alex into the living room. The fireplace made the room nice and toasty.

Her father rose from the couch and extended his hand. "I'm Bill Riley, Kate's dad."

"Nice to meet you, sir."

Kate's mother came into the living room, drying her hands on her festive Christmas apron. "Hello, you must be Alex. I'm Isla, Kate's mom."

"Hello, Mrs. Riley."

"Please, Isla and Bill. There aren't any formalities with Kate's boyfriend. You must be exhausted from your flight. Kate will show you to her room. Would you like a cup of coffee or hot chocolate?"

"Mom, Alex can stay in the guest bedroom." Kate turned to him. "I asked my mom to set it up. It's really comfortable."

"Oh, no, honey. Don't be silly… we're all adults here."

"Since when, Mom?"

"Oh honey, you and Alex can both stay in your old room." Kate stared at her mother. *What? Since when did she become a free spirit? Ten years ago, she was a prude. Now she's free and wild and it's we're all adults here.*

"Thanks, Mrs. Riley… I mean Isla, and yes, coffee sounds good." Alex curled his fingers around Kate's waist, tugging her into his body. "See, honey, you thought we would have to sneak off." He kissed her brow.

Kate narrowed her eyes at him, but he ignored her.

"Go on, you two. I'll have the coffee ready in the kitchen."

Alex retrieved his suitcase from the foyer and followed Kate up the stairs to her bedroom. He closed the door to Kate's room. She went over to the bed and pulled the Christmas comforter off and spread it on the floor at the foot of the bed.

Alex glanced at the comforter and then to the bed. "You know that we're both adults and not adolescents. I'm sure we can be comfortable in your bed without either of us…" He grinned. "Unless… you can't control yourself."

"Me? Believe me, I won't be jumping on you. I can control myself just as well as the next person. For your information, I haven't been with anyone since my ex—"

She blurted that out without meaning to. She felt her cheeks flush at the spark from his emerald-green eyes before she turned away.

"Well, then I'd say we'll be all right not jumping onto each other… unless we both agree… to adding some spice to our fake dating arrangement," he said in a husky voice.

Why hadn't she heard how deep his voice was? He laughed, and Kate realized she liked the sound of his laugh. Actually, she liked him.

"We could see… if we want to add more to the relationship."

"Keep it in your pants, buddy, and we can get through this," she added with a slight smile.

"I hope you don't mind the explosion of Christmas in the house. My mom spends days decorating. Even the en suite is decorated. As for me, I have no decorations in my condo in Santa Monica, not even an artificial tree," Kate said as she made room in her closet for Alex.

"I like all the decorations. It reminds me of my childhood. My mother was the same. Decorating every room in the house," he said, while unzipping his garment bag.

Then she emptied a drawer in her dresser. "I'll give you a shelf in the medicine cabinet for your shaving gear." *Does he have condoms in his… what am I thinking?*

"Thanks," he said as he hung two suits and a tuxedo in her closet. "I rented a car so that you and I don't need to rely on anyone to drive us to all of the outings your family has planned."

"I'm glad you did that. Olivia suggested that you and I go in the same car with Dan and Brittany." She tried to keep the anger and frustration from her voice as she said, "I can't understand why she keeps pushing me toward them." *The woman stole my husband.*

Alex held her shoulders, and she gazed up at him. "I'm here to make sure you don't have to deal with them and make Dan regret his choice."

"Your pants are buzzing." She tried for humor.

The corners of his mouth lifted into a smile, gradually showing his even, white teeth. "I just received a text." He pulled his phone from his pocket and glanced at the screen. "It's from the rental car company. The car will be here before we go to dinner this evening. I rented a two-seater sports car."

"Perfect," she said. "No room for anyone but us."

"Exactly what I was thinking."

That night, Alex wore a dark-blue suit with a crisp white-silk shirt and blue-striped tie. Kate chose a black velvet skirt with an emerald-green silk blouse tucked into the waistband. The color matched Alex's eyes exactly. It couldn't have been better if she planned it. Everyone would think she did.

Kate chose to wear her very high heels, and on her ears, diamond studs that she'd bought for herself after her divorce. No rings or any other adornments.

Alex turned to her. "You look beautiful. Are you ready to wow them?"

"I'm so nervous about getting caught in a lie. I hope I don't spoil it."

"Lean on me, and I'll get you through this. Focus on the reason we're doing this."

They walked into the living room. Christmas music played in the background, and the small group chatted and mingled. Her father stood at the bar, preparing drinks. Her mother brought out a Christmas serving tray filled with appetizers. Fried mozzarella, tiny individual bite-size pizzas, and triangle-shaped spanakopita filled the tray. The spinach artichoke dip and crackers were on a sideboard, along with a creamy jalapeño dip with chips, and sliced green and red bell peppers for dipping. Her father's favorite blue cheese dip with celery sticks was on a raised plate in the center. On another sideboard were Christmas cocktail napkins and tiny appetizer plates and serving utensils. It looked to Kate as if her mother bought out the snack aisle at the local supermarket.

"My mom loves Christmas and has collected three separate china patterns, one for dining, one for cocktails, and one for breakfast and lunch. She's an over-achiever, just like me," Kate said to Alex.

Olivia and Ben mingled among the guests, laughing and joking. Her sister looked radiant in a white-velvet, skintight dress and her strawberry-blond hair loose around her shoulders. Pearl stud earrings and a single-strand pearl necklace were all she wore, other than her two-karat round diamond engagement ring.

Kate's ex-in-laws were there. Her ex-father-in-law was talking with her dad, and her ex-mother-in-law came over. "Kate, when Olivia told me you were definitely coming for the engagement party, I was thrilled." She tugged Kate in for a hug.

"Mo… Mrs. Thompson, it's nice to see you. Allow me to introduce Dr. Alexander Messina, my boyfriend."

Alex shook the elder woman's hand. "A pleasure to meet you."

"Thank you, Doctor Messina." She turned to Kate. "I'm sad that you can't call me mom anymore."

"Mrs. Thompson, you were wonderful to me, and you know that you will always have a special place in my heart." Kate hugged the woman and kissed her on her cheek.

Dan and Brittany sat in a corner, quietly chatting with Olivia and Ben. Dan doted on his wife, bringing her sparkling water and some of the healthier snacks. Brittany placed her hand on his thigh. Kate felt the knot in her stomach tighten.

"Kiss, kiss, kiss, you're under the mistletoe. Kiss, kiss," chanted Kate's mother. Kate looked up. *Of course.* She and Alex were standing under the mistletoe.

"Shall we?" Alex asked.

Kate nodded, and he enfolded her in his masculine arms. He tightened one around her shoulders and one around her waist. The look in his gaze said, I told you we should have practiced this.

Her heart fluttered as his lips reached hers. *Oh, my. I hope*

I... Ahh. The soft brush of his lips against hers made her melt into him. His spicy, delectable scent drifted around her. All she wanted was to feel more of the pressure of his sculpted lips. He was definitely good at this. What would he think of her kiss? His arms tightened around her, and there was no more shouting, no more family or anyone. Nothing but Alex kissing her and his husky voice low and soft. *OMG did he tell me I was his wet dream?* She surrendered to the passion of his kiss, never before feeling like this.

Alex broke the kiss. The sexual haze that engulfed Kate gradually lifted, and she remembered that they were standing in the middle of her parents' living room. She composed herself, hiding her shock at her response to the touch of his lips.

Alex kept his hand on her waist as she introduced him to Ben. Ignoring Dan and Brittany, she led him to her dad.

Plans were discussed for the days leading up to the gala engagement party. Tomorrow would be cookie baking and tree decorating at Dan and Brittany's.

That came as a surprise to Kate. "I thought we were baking here."

"My future brother-in-law..." Olivia giggled. "And my future sister-in-law want to contribute to the festivities, so they volunteered their house. Then we want to help decorate their tree with them."

"Oh, I see how it's going to be," Kate snarked.

"Olivia thought of all these activities, and the couple's only rule," Brittany said, throwing her sister under the bus.

"That figures," Kate said, holding in her anger.

"I'm so happy that you have a plus one for the next four days," Olivia gushed.

Kate knew in her own selfish way that Olivia was trying to smooth everything over. It was an impossible situation.

Alex curled his fingers around Kate's waist as he held her

close to him. "We're going to miss cookie baking and tree decorating, I'm afraid. I don't have much time before I have to return to L.A., so I'm taking Kate out. A special day for just the two of us." He brushed his lips against her brow. "Isn't that right, my love?"

"Yes, darling. Just you and me." She rose on her toes and kissed him.

"We had better get going to the restaurant. We have an eight thirty dinner reservation at the Sea Port Inn," Kate's dad said.

"Mom, Dad, Alex and I will lock up for you and then meet all of you at the restaurant."

"Oh, thank you, both," Isla said.

The restaurant was popular and always crowded, but the large group sat in a semi-private area designated just for the Riley-Thompson party. Their tables overlooked the dance floor, and they would certainly be able to dance during dinner. Dan and his very pregnant wife Brittany sat next to Ben, while Kate and Alex sat next to Olivia.

"To the happy couple, cheers," Ben's father said. Others chimed in and more toasts were made.

"Let's dance," Alex said. He led Kate onto the restaurant's intimate dance floor.

She whispered, "We didn't discuss dancing on the plane."

Alex held her hand and as he slipped his arm around her waist, he laid her hand against his chest. "Let's see if we can pull it off." He spun her into the first steps of a waltz.

"I'm happy to say that my dance lessons paid off. You're great." Kate smiled and gazed into his emerald-green eyes. His smile dazzled her as he spun her around.

He was her best fake date ever. Okay, maybe her only fake date, but definitely the best. He made her forget Dan and Brittany and for a moment, Kate thought maybe this could be real. "I can't remember the last time I've been out dancing," she whispered as she laid her head on his shoulder. He held her tighter. "I know it's fake, but Alex, it feels so right."

He brushed his lips on her cheek. "Yes, it does… feel very real."

They stayed on the dance floor for two more slow dances, and then the party was ready to go.

Alex and Kate held hands as they walked to the cloak room to get their coats. Olivia came up behind them and said, "We came with Dan and Brittany. They're dropping us at our apartment."

The air was brisk, and Kate wrapped her coat around her. Alex put his arm around her waist and said, "The car should be here soon. We're both used to the milder L.A. weather."

When the Ferrari was brought to the curb, Alex helped Kate into the car.

Dan said, "Wow, you rented a Ferrari! That must cost at least a grand a day." Alex didn't answer. Instead, he tipped the valet and slid behind the wheel. He grinned at the group, shifted the car into gear, and drove away.

"OMG Alex, that was the best. To see their faces was priceless. You're the best fake date, thinking of all these little details. I love it."

CHAPTER 5

All through the evening, Alex noticed how uncomfortable and uneasy Kate was around Olivia, Dan, and Brittany. Especially when Brittany touched Dan. In the car and on the drive home, he felt her relax. Her features became more animated as they spoke. When they arrived home from the restaurant, they went right up to her room.

She asked him, "So, what are we going to do tomorrow?"

He browsed through the clothes in her closet. "Can I see what you're wearing to the engagement party."

"I have something."

"Let me see." He hadn't seen anything ball worthy in her closet when he snooped.

Kate leaned into her closet and pulled out a very cute, off-the-shoulder, lace cocktail dress. She held it to her, and Alex cupped his chin and tapped his pointing finger over his lips. Then he shook his head and said, "It's very pretty. One evening, I'd like to see you in it, but…" He shook his head. "I don't think this will do for your sister's engagement party."

Kate held the beige dress to her and looked in the full-length standing mirror. "No? I was being practical. I know I can be boring at times."

"I don't believe you can ever bore me, not even when I'm ninety and going feeble. So, if we're going to wow them all, you'll save practical for another time. Tomorrow, first thing, we go to Saks and then maybe catch the matinee at Radio City."

Her eyes rounded. "The Christmas Spectacular? I haven't gone in years."

"We can also get a glimpse of the tree. It's lit from—"

"Six a.m. until midnight each day," she said with a giggle in her voice. "New Yorker, born and bred. Remember?"

She was such an imp and a seductress all rolled up into one. That kiss they shared under the mistletoe—he wanted more. When she stepped into his body and molded herself to him, he had to break the kiss and stop himself from lifting her lethal body into his arms and carrying her off to bed.

"We can have dinner out before we drive home."

She frowned at him, shaking her head. "Everything up until dinner is perfect. Tomorrow is paella night, so if we can be home for that, then I love your plans. I like your way of thinking, Doctor Messina. Yes, that will be much better than my sister's plan."

Kate rolled the Christmas comforter into a bolster and placed it down the middle over the red blanket of the queen-size bed. Then she went into the en suite, holding her nightgown.

While she was in the other room, Alex stripped to his boxers and got into bed. Kate ran across the room and hurried under the covers. They each lay on their side of the barrier. Kate pulled the blanket over her shoulder. "Good night, Alex."

"Night, beautiful." He listened to Kate's even breath as she fell off to sleep. Alex lay on his back, massaged the tension from his neck, and tried not to think of the glimpse of curves he got when Kate slid under the covers. Her sexy nightgown could easily be slipped from her body... the red-satin nightgown...

Beads of sweat broke out on his forehead. He was as hard as a rock. Kate had rolled over the barrier, and her soft lips brushed his neck. Her breasts rubbed his chest, and he groaned at the torture chamber that her bedroom had become.

"Kate, wake up," he whispered. "If you don't move off me, I can't be held responsible for how this ends."

"Mmm... okay..." She snuggled closer. "You smell so good," she said and kissed his neck.

Her wildflower scent clung to her skin, driving him crazy. Kate slid her naked leg up over his bare thighs as she sprinkled kisses over his chest. "Alex..." She rose and straddled him.

"Kate," he groaned. "Last chance to stop this."

In the glow of the Christmas lights from the window, he saw that she was sleeping. The room had turned into an inferno, his own personal hell. "Kate."

Her silken voice caressed him. "Kiss me like you did under the mistletoe. I've never felt like that before." She pressed her soft lips to his and slipped her tongue into his mouth.

The intense need of her kiss set his soul on fire. He needed to memorize the texture of her lips and the taste of her tongue. He could kiss her forever, and it wouldn't be enough.

She sucked on his tongue. *Oh God, control, man.* He wrapped his arms around her waist, pressing on the firm flesh of her buttocks. Her nightgown had ridden up, and she moaned into his mouth.

He felt her shift and gasp as she woke up. "Oh, Alex, I'm sorry."

Kate rolled off him, and he cursed at his stupidity. If he'd kept his mouth shut, they would have been making love right now, but no, he had to be noble.

"I'm so sorry. I… I… was asleep," she groaned.

He rolled to his side and rested his head in the palm of his hand. "Now that you're awake, what do you say to our finishing what you started." He smiled at her.

She sat up and pushed the lustrous black tresses from her face. "No, I mean, I'm sorry that happened. It won't ever again. I'll sleep in the guest room." She grabbed her pillow.

"What will your mother say when she finds out we aren't sharing a room, let alone the bed."

She groaned and in a small voice, she said, "Okay, but I can't trust you."

"Me. You were the one on top of me. In another minute, we wouldn't be having this conversation. We would have been having sex."

"Yes, sex, nothing more." She faced away from him and pulled the cover over her shoulder.

He had a difficult time falling back to sleep. He thought of Kate and her hot, seductive mouth. What would her mouth feel like on his dick? How would making love to her feel? When she straddled him, and he felt the heat between her legs on his abdomen… What had he gotten himself into? He liked her, that was for sure, and wanted to help her. He didn't want to go to Sicily, and he didn't want to spend another Christmas alone. When she talked about all the Christmas activities, he couldn't help himself. There was a twinge of loneliness in him, but there was more to it—feelings he thought long dead came to the surface. He wanted her and not just for sex. He liked her from the moment she sat next to him on the plane. In the brief time they knew each other, he'd wanted to get to know more about her. That never happened before. How could he have just let her fly under the radar into his heart? She had no idea how beautiful she was. What a seductress she was.

34

CHAPTER 6

The next morning, Kate tried not to think about what happened in the middle of the night. She visualized his washboard abs. She tried to blame Alex, although the lawyer in her knew the evidence was clear. She was on top of him, sucking his tongue into her mouth. She ignored the zing of desire that settled between her legs. *Oh, if he would put his tongue right there and licked my clit.* She stopped the erotic thoughts spinning out of control and went into the en suite. *Maybe I should break down and buy a vibrator?* Kate showered and dressed for their outing. She wore a silk shell under her cashmere cable knit sweater and her straight-leg wool pants. She slid her feet into her ankle boots and draped her Teddy Bear coat over her arm. Another expensive purchase for this trip, she would show them she didn't need a husband and could make it on her own. All color coordinated, she was ready. *I don't have to prove anything to anyone, but I just need to.*

Kate walked into the kitchen cheery and with a spring in her step. "Good morning." She kissed her mom. "Mmmm, your cooking smells delicious already."

"Morning, beautiful. Where's my kiss?" Alex asked.

Kate's cheeks flushed as she remembered last night. Alex strode over to her, dressed in navy-blue pants and a light-blue, long-sleeve shirt. Over that, he wore a crewneck cashmere pullover sweater. He wore leather loafers, and his spicy cologne subtly drifted around her.

"Good morning." Kate lifted her brow to Alex, then tipped her head, offering her cheek. He shook his head and opened his arms. Kate pecked him on his freshly shaven cheek.

"That's a kiss for an old man, not your boyfriend," Isla said.

"You're so right, Isla," Alex said as he walked back to his seat, holding Kate's hand. He tugged her onto his lap. *Yummy, he's so handsome.* Kate kissed Alex on his lips.

"Better, Mom?" she said, continuing to sit on his lap. Alex kissed her neck. Her heart jolted, and her nipples tightened.

"Hey, what's going on here?" her dad said.

"Mom is critiquing my kissing." Kate pushed her bottom lip forward in a pout.

"Oh, really, Isla."

Kate wiggled off Alex's lap. "Can we help?" She tried to hide her discomfort.

Alex sipped his coffee.

"Are you hungry? Maybe you can prepare breakfast for you and Alex."

"Yes, I can. How about you, Dad?"

"No, sweetie. Your mother and I had breakfast earlier. I'll be in my office." He shook Alex's hand. "You two have fun in the city."

"What would you like for breakfast," Kate asked.

Isla said, "I'm sure you've had Kate's hash browns? They are the best."

"Are you holding out on me, beautiful?"

"No… but… well—"

"It's okay, your mother isn't naive. Isla, we're usually running in the morning. Most mornings, I'm in the O.R. by six a.m., so I don't have time for breakfast. Kate hasn't cooked for me yet."

"Well, you're in for a treat."

"Not today, Mom. We're in a rush. Just coffee and a muffin for me."

"Don't forget I'm making paella for this evening." To Alex, she said, "It's our family tradition."

"No, Mom, I didn't. Does that mean there's an ugly sweater contest on the horizon?"

Isla smiled and shook her head.

"Mom makes paella from a family recipe handed down from her great-grandmother."

"I like paella. I had it when I was in Spain. Can we help you?" Alex asked as he placed his empty cup and plate in the sink.

"Thank you, Alex, but you two go enjoy the day. I like to prepare this meal with my husband."

"Knowing them, the dining room table is already set with my mom's favorite Christmas china and all her fancy silver and crystal stemware."

He smiled, then said, "That sounds really nice."

Kate took one more sip of coffee, then rinsed her and Alex's cup and plate. She put them in the dishwasher. "We're going now," she said as she dried her hands on a snowman hand towel.

"Can you be back by eight for dinner and ugly sweater contest?"

"Yes." On the side to Alex, she whispered, "See, I told you at least one contest, maybe two."

He laughed. "I'm going to have to buy a sweater while we're out. Let's go shopping first."

"Are we going to Saks?"

"Yes, then we can walk to Radio City. Maybe have lunch before the matinee."

He drove into Manhattan, reminding Kate that although Alex lived in Bel Air and had a practice in Beverly Hills, he'd grown up in New York. Even went to medical school in New York; not until later did he move to L.A.

Alex found a parking garage near Sixth Avenue and West 51st Street to park the rented Ferrari. He'd taken her hand as they walked toward Saks. She felt a thrill at the touch of his fingers as they entwined with hers. They walked down to Fifth Avenue and as they passed St. Patrick's Cathedral, organ music spilled onto the street.

It was mid-morning, and the streets were crowded with traffic. Car horns blared at pedestrians as they ran across the street. Kate liked the hustle and bustle of New York at Christmas. People walking on the sidewalks, some carrying shopping bags filled with wrapped presents. Some people were looking in the store windows, at the festive decorations and listening to the merry music.

There was excitement in the air. Tourists snapping photos and selfies in front of the store windows. Kate said, "You can always spot the New Yorkers. They're the ones looking straight ahead and not up at the buildings."

"Yes, and they aren't taking pictures," he said and led her through the main doors of the famous department store. "Kate, let's pick out a dress first. Then we'll see if you need anything else. I see a collection of ugly sweaters near the escalators. We can pick up one on the way out."

The store wasn't crowded. Kate draped her coat over her shoulders, and they found the designer formal wear. "I like the dress on that mannequin. It's green, my favorite color." *Like your eyes.*

"I liked the green blouse you wore last night, but what

about this one?" Alex pointed to another mannequin. "I think you'll knock them dead in the red one. It will hug you in all the right places."

"You seem to know a lot about fashion." *And women.*

"No, just what I like," he said, gazing into her eyes.

A sales associate asked if there were anything they would like to see.

"We would like an evening gown. Perhaps this one," Alex said.

"Yes. That one in a size six. Will you be able to ship it locally today?" Kate asked.

"Yes, of course," the clerk said.

Kate tried on the dress, and it fit her like a glove. The rouching over her torso accented her curves and the floor-length gown was styled with a mermaid skirt, flaring past her knees. She stepped onto a platform in front of a three-sided mirror.

Alex came over. "You're definitely going to wow them," he whispered. "Brittany will turn green when she sees you."

The associate touched the hem and said, "Do you have a higher pair of heels?"

Kate giggled. "And not ankle boots? I do actually have a pair of strappy gold stilettos I can wear."

"Then you won't need any alterations. It fits you perfect and with the high heels, the length will be just right," the associate said.

Alex reached into his pocket. "I have an account here—"

Kate turned to the associate and said, "Will you excuse us for a moment?"

"Certainly, miss."

Kate whispered to Alex, "What do you think you're doing?"

He bent and said, "Buying you a dress."

"I appreciate the thought, Alex, but I can buy my own dress."

"I know you can, but would it be so bad if I wanted to buy the most beautiful woman I know this dress?"

His words and the fire in his eyes sent a zing of excitement through her. "You're doing so much for me. I'll buy the dress."

The red gown was wrapped and once they chose an ugly sweater on the main floor, their purchases would be couriered to Long Island later today.

When they left the department store across the street from Rockefeller Center, Kate said, "Would you think I was ungrateful if we went ice skating instead of going to see the Christmas show today? I've never skated here."

"Ungrateful, how? You wouldn't let me buy you the gown..." He frowned at her. "You've never skated here? My grandparents brought Caroline and me here all the time to twirl around at the rink."

"You did say that your grandparents raised you and your sister. But now they live in Palermo?"

Alex slipped his arm around Kate's waist as they walked toward Rockefeller Center. "My father was born in Sicily, and while he was on a business trip to New York, he met my mother. They fell in love and got married. She didn't want to leave New York, so my father moved here and started a new life with my mother."

Kate gazed up at him. "That's so nice, but how did you end up being raised by your grandparents?"

Alex slowed his step, and Kate could see a sadness come over him. "I'm sorry, Alex. I shouldn't have asked. I didn't realize this would be a sad subject... you don't need to tell me."

He'd stopped walking and turned to her. "It will always be tragic, but the pain is less... I was twelve and visiting my grandparents in Sicily. My parents and Caroline were in a car accident. Caroline was thrown from the car, and my parents died instantly. Caroline suffered multiple injuries."

Kate hugged him. "Oh Alex, I'm so sorry. Don't say any more."

They began walking again and passed a concession stand. "Want a coffee or hot chocolate before we rent the skates?" Alex asked.

"I want whatever will make you happy. We don't have to stay. Let's go see the show instead."

"Kate, I'm good with this. I have happy memories here. Caroline is the reason I became a plastic surgeon. She needed multiple reconstructive facial surgeries. Her doctor was great and later, when I graduated from medical school, I was able to intern with him."

"Your grandparents stayed in the United States to raise you both?"

"Yes, my grandfather worked with the Italian Diplomatic Corps. He was fortunate enough to transfer to the Italian Embassy here in Manhattan." They walked to the ticket office as they spoke, and Alex bought the entry ticket and skate rental coupons.

They were able to join the next session on the ice. The festive holiday music hummed through her as Alex led her around the rink.

"I'm a little wobbly on the skates, but you know what you're doing," she said.

His arm tightened around her waist. "I won't let you fall."

"Thanks. I do feel safe in your arms, dancing... skating..." *Kissing, maybe more.*

They went around the rink another time, then he went a little faster.

"Oh no, Alex, I'm going to fall."

"Hang onto me."

She sighed. "You're the boss." And held on to him.

"That's exactly what I want to hear." He smiled at her.

All Kate could think of was his lips on hers and how it would feel to run her tongue along his bottom lip. He caught her as she lost her balance, bringing her tighter to his side, preventing her from falling.

"When the session is over, let's go up the Rock to the observation decks."

"Yes, another place I've never been."

Once they finished skating and changed back into their shoes, they took the elevator up seventy floors to one of the three observation decks. "I never grow tired of this." Alex said, extending his hand to take in the 360-degree view.

They found an unoccupied area on the enclosed deck with a view of the Empire State Building directly in front of them. Kate stuffed her hat into her pocket, and Alex stood behind her. He wrapped his arms around her waist, and she leaned into his broad chest.

Kate relaxed into him and said, "I love New York City, and I miss my parents, but I'm happy that I live in L.A. I was just promoted at the law firm, and I'm finally settling into becoming a West Coast girl.

He kissed the top of her head, and Kate turned to gaze into his eyes. "I'm thrilled that you live in the same city I do," he said, tugging her tighter to his muscular frame. "You'll have to tell me more about your promotion, and your career. It must be exciting to be a trial attorney. Speaking of careers, tomorrow, I'll need to do some work."

"I'm sorry I've taken you from your patients."

"I need a private place to have a virtual consult and catch up on my emails. Check in with some patients."

"I'm sure my father will let you use his office. It's very private; it's connected to the main house, but above the garage."

They rode the elevator to the ground floor and then walked toward the parking garage.

Kate said, "If we get on the expressway before three thirty, we can beat rush-hour traffic back home."

Alex nodded and as they walked past a pretzel cart, he said, "Those pretzels smell delicious. What do you say, shall we indulge?"

"Yes, I haven't had one of those in years."

Alex bought two huge, warm pretzels from the vendor. They both tore off pieces and ate as they walked back to the Ferrari.

JUST BEFORE THEY came down to dinner, Kate said, "My parents give out trophies in three different categories. Best couple, best male, and best female in the ugliest sweater they can find."

Alex chuckled. "Well, what we picked isn't really ugly but perfect for a couple in love."

"I hope we can pull that part off. I'm glad you convinced me to wear this instead." Kate ran her hand down a white, long-sleeve snowman sweater dress that ended mid-thigh. The bodice was the face, two eyes, a carrot nose, and a smile. Tied around her waist was a green and red color-block knit scarf with red and green fringe. On her stomach were three black dots. Kate wore her black ankle boots to complete the look.

Alex wore a snowman sweater to match Kate's outfit. They walked into the living room holding hands. Olivia saw them first and exclaimed. "Oh, I know who's going to win best couple. You guys look great."

"Nice, very nice," Ben said as he shook Alex's hand.

Then she and Alex walked over to the bar. "My parents

make homemade sangria to go with dinner. Would you like a glass?"

"Yes, my love." Kate poured, and they sat on the couch, chatting about their day in the city and listening to the others talk about baking and tree decorating. They all waited for her parents to judge the contest. Olivia was right Kate and Alex won best couple. Ben won best male and Brittany won best female. Once it was over, they went to the dining room where they waited for Kate's dad to make a grand entrance, carrying in the enormous platter filled with layers of yellow rice, meat, vegetables, and seafood.

While they all enjoyed the paella, Dan's cell phone rang. "Oh, I apologize, but I have to take this call." He stepped into the other room. The rest of the conversation continued.

Brittany said, "Dan has been trying to get tickets to a show that's been sold out for over a year."

"I know he asked me if I had any friends that may know a way to get two tickets," Ben said.

Mr. Riley added, "It's not only that the show is sold out, but the tickets are fifteen hundred a piece!"

Dan walked back into the dining room. "Sorry, everyone. Honey, I couldn't get the tickets. I'm sorry, not even into the new year. It's completely sold out."

"What show is it?" Alex asked. "There are a few right now that are sold out."

"Only the hottest show—Merlin and Morgana."

"Oh, I'm taking Kate to the eight o'clock performance tomorrow."

Kate clapped her hands. "Oh honey, is that the surprise you have for me?"

"Part of it." He curled his arm around her shoulder.

"I'm so excited. How did you know I wanted to go?" Kate turned toward Alex.

"I have my ways." He slid his hand to her waist.

Kate leaned toward him and kissed Alex. "You really are Santa," she whispered loud enough for all to hear.

"Santa?" Olivia said.

"Yes, a private joke between Alex and me."

Later that night, when they went up to her room, she hugged Alex and couldn't help herself as she burst out laughing. "That was good the way you thought to say we had tickets to the play."

He kissed her brow. "I do have tickets. I didn't when I said it, but I called the show's producer. His wife is a patient of mine, and tomorrow for the eight o'clock performance, there will be two tickets for us at the box office. He's sending a limousine, so we can also go to dinner before and drinks after." He held her to him.

Her jaw dropped before she squealed with delight and bounced on her toes. "Oh, you are the best." She looped her arms around his neck and leaned into his muscular body.

"Can I get a kiss?" His husky voice sent shivers up her spine.

"Yes." *And more if you want.* Kate rose on her toes and moved her hands up to his cheeks. She opened her lips to the touch of his and kissed him with an overwhelming hunger, knowing there was only one conclusion to the searing heat of their lips. Kate molded herself to Alex's hard body.

He took control as his hands reached up to cradle her head. Nipping at her bottom lip, his kiss was hot and demanding, and Kate pressed her lips more firmly to his with her own set of demands. She moaned in delight when his tongue slid inside her mouth to entwine with hers. Her pulse raced and in an instant, she was wet and hot for him.

Alex slid a hand to her buttocks, pressing her closer to him. Her breath hitched at the feel of his desire. She inhaled his peppery, zesty scent. She dug her fingers into his shoulders. He made her hunger for more.

"Alex…" She pushed the hem of his sweater up, and he lifted his arms. The kiss broke for a second, and she cried at the loss.

He went back to kissing and touching her. She unbuttoned his shirt, tugging the tails from his pants. Alex pushed the hem of her dress up past her waist. The heat of his hand stroked her naked torso. Then he cupped her breast and pinched her nipple through the lace of her bra.

It was too much and not enough. She needed more. This time, she broke the kiss long enough to rid herself of her snowman dress. *Thank God I wore my sexy bra and panties.* Her body burned at his gaze. His eyes shot sparks of green fire into her core, igniting an uncontrollable need in her. The sound of his zipper sent tingles up her spine. Slipping her hand into his silk boxers, she stroked his powerful erection.

Alex shook his head. "Keep your hands at your sides if you want this to last."

He kissed the tip of her nose, and his fingers found the hooks of her bra. Her breasts felt swollen, aching for his hands and his mouth. He whisked the bra from her, and his thumb and forefinger teased a nipple into a tight bud. A whoosh of burning heat settled between her legs.

Alex moved his mouth over her other nipple, tracing the bud with his tongue before sucking it into his mouth. *Oh, God, yes, yes, yes.*

ALEX KNELT in front of Kate's lethal body; never before had he needed to taste a woman the way he needed her. He tugged her lace panties past her knees and breathed in her scent.

She shivered.

Heat settled in his groin.

"Alex, I'm not a woman of the world." Her voice quivered.

He lifted his gaze to her. "Kate, you say no, and I stop."

"I was married, but I'm not—

Her beauty and passion overwhelmed him as his dick throbbed. Alex rose to his feet, lifted her in his arms, and carried her to bed. He laid her in the center of the bed and kissed her lips, then he nipped the bow of her top lip. Feathery soft, his hands explored her body. He memorized her lips, gently coaxing her to slide her tiny tongue into his mouth. Kate moaned, digging her fingers into his hair. She explored his mouth, entwining her tongue with his. She sighed.

To have her in his arms, desire raced through his veins, but he went slow, cupping her breast. He thrilled when Kate pushed herself into his hand. The feel of her nipple tightening against his palm sent jolts of pleasure through him. He kissed her taut nipple, tracing a path into the valley between her breasts, taking her other nipple into his mouth, sucking, and licking.

Kate writhed against him, holding his head to her and pressing her breast into his mouth. "Oh, Alex...yes, so good." She tugged him to her body.

He kissed her breasts, into the valley of her cleavage, and down her torso. Alex licked a path over her satin-smooth skin to her belly. He gazed up. Her black hair spread across the pillow in lustrous waves before curling around her. Her eyes were closed, the column of her neck arched, her pert breasts, wet from his mouth, rose and fell with the excited panting of her breath.

"Kate, look at me." He slipped his palm up to her breasts and down her rib cage, with his fingers splayed over her quivering abdomen.

She gazed into his eyes. "Oh, Alex," she moaned. "Yes." Her thighs fell open.

He nuzzled the inside of one silken thigh and then the other. The dark curls glistened with her need. Alex slipped his hands under the firmness of her buttocks, lifting her to his lips. His thumbs spread her, so he could intimately kiss her before he opened his mouth, drinking in her wild, hot taste.

Kate whimpered.

The taste of her desire drove him to explore her folds, sucking and licking before he sheathed his tongue in her core. He thrust his tongue into her liquid heat over and over again. Beautiful, sweet Kate arched into him, and he licked her clit, teasing the bud with the tip of his tongue, adding pressure with the flat of his tongue. Her fingers dug into his hair, stroking his head. She curled her pelvis, offering all of herself to his mouth. *God, I love her.*

His years of experience paid off. All he wanted to do was please this woman. He used his erotic skill, stretching and curling his tongue as he found her G-spot.

"Alex, Alex… ahhh, yes." She rocked her sex against his mouth. Her thighs quivered, and her fingers dug into his hair as she held him to her. Her breath hitched as she shuddered and pulsed on his tongue.

He watched her lift her hand to muffle her scream of pleasure. He drove her wild with his tongue. Her cheeks were flushed, her arm flung across the pillow, and her breath panted out of her. Alex crawled up her sensuous body. "Ready for more?"

"Yes, I want all of you." Kate spread her thighs. Her fingers curled around his shoulders.

Alex grabbed the foil packet he'd placed on the bedside table. "Do I need this?"

She nodded. "Let me help you."

She was a contradiction, driving him crazy. He kissed her

brow before he rolled the protection on. Alex rested the head of his erection at her opening.

Kate wrapped her arms around his neck. "Yes, now." She kissed his chest, licked his flat nipples, and ran her hand down his back.

"Put your legs around me. I can't wait another minute to be in your hot pussy."

She clung to him. "Mmmm… Yes, Alex, now. Don't wait." She moved under him.

He thrust in, sliding deep into the tight heat. "Kate." He groaned at the exquisite pleasure.

She lifted her leg, and the heel of her foot dug into his back. He pushed deeper into her wet heat. Her hips rose to meet him. His hips pressed forward, and he buried himself to the hilt, savoring the feel of her pulsing, quaking core.

She lifted her hips once more. "Alex, please."

He met her plea, thrusting into her tight, wet core. Her inner walls rippled against him, and he pistoned harder, faster.

Kate wrapped her legs around his waist. "Yes, yes." Her head fell back onto the pillow, and her sooty lashes covered her eyes.

No woman had ever felt so good, been so wild. With a roar of satisfaction, he covered her mouth to catch her screams of pleasure, as they came together.

CHAPTER 7

The bolster had been thrown to the floor in the night as Alex wrapped his arms around Kate's naked body, holding her against him. She snuggled into him, and he kissed the soft spot behind her ear and down her neck, his lips gliding over her silken shoulder.

"Mmmm, good morning." She rolled over in his arms. "It wasn't a dream; you're really here." She parted her lips and kissed him. "What time is it? It's still dark outside."

"Six, too early for you? I have to do some work."

"But it's three in the morning in L.A.," She kissed his stubble-covered jaw.

He brushed his hand over her breast, watching as her nipple extended. "Jumping to conclusions again? I'm going to be consulting with someone in France. Then I'm going to check on my emails. By that time, I can call my office and see if there is anything more I need to take care of. Your dad said I can use his office whenever I needed, so I have to get started."

"Oh," was all she said. "I don't know why I said that.

Would it be jumping to conclusions if I thought we were going to make love right now?"

He groaned. Kate was so soft and warm from sleep. Alex nibbled on the breast he'd been fondling. He pressed his arousal against her silken thigh. "What do you think?"

"Yesss, yes, yes, no conclusion, but the real thing," she whispered.

His hand slipped down over her belly to caress her; his finger stroked the black tuff of hair, questing for more. Her moan filled him with a need to satisfy her. He found her clit and rubbed his finger around the bud. It grew slippery to his touch.

She moaned his name.

He would never grow tired of the sounds she made or his name on her lips. He parted her legs with his knee. "Kate, I need you."

"Yes, Alex." Her fingers wrapped around him, and she guided his head into her wet heat. She moved under him as he thrust into her tight passage. Kate gripped his biceps, lifting her leg. Alex caught her knee in the crook of his elbow.

"Yes, more, more." She lifted her other leg.

He guided her leg to his shoulder and thrust into her. Pulling almost completely out, he plunged into her again and again. She mewled as her pussy stroked his dick, drawing an orgasm from him as the waves of her own clenched him. As their breath returned to normal, Alex stroked her lustrous dark hair from her face, kissing her brow. She snuggled to him. "I like morning sex with you."

"Me too," he said, before he slipped from the bed.

Kate snuggled under the covers as she watched Alex walk to the en suite. His muscles rippled across his broad shoulders, his narrow waist, and marble-hard butt. He reminded her of the statute of David she'd seen in Florence the summer she graduated from college. Kate stretched, and her body felt delightfully sore. She threw the cover off and rose from the bed.

While Alex was in the shower, Kate turned on the sink faucet and picked up a washcloth and a bar of soap. She squealed when his hand snaked out from the shower curtain and grabbed her. He hauled her into the tight space with him. "I think we can manage in here, but wait until I get you into my shower at home." He bent to kiss her and lifted her into his arms.

Kate wrapped her legs around his narrow hips, the warm water beat on her back. "Alex... I've never..."

He kissed her, and she wrapped her arms around his neck, holding onto him as he held her buttocks in his powerful hands. He thrust into her.

She gripped his shoulders, feeling safe in his arms. He lifted her and lowered her onto his enormous erection. Her body clenched around him as her head tilted back. He licked her neck, kissed her breasts, and impaled her on his hot hard as steel erection. A wild orgasm ripped through her. She shuddered in pleasure, screaming his name.

Alex smiled and stayed buried deep in her pulsing core. She rested her head in the crook of his shoulder, and he lifted and lowered her on his shaft as pleasure sizzled through her. She came once more in quivering waves. Kate coaxed Alex toward his own climax. He gritted his teeth, pulled out, and spilled his hot seed.

"I love shower sex," she said as her legs slid down his thighs.

"Wait until we try making love in my whirlpool tub."

"Oh, I like that idea."

He wrapped a towel around his waist. "We have the show tonight. Tomorrow is Christmas Eve and the engagement party. When do you fly back to L.A?"

Kate had dried herself and now stepped into a pair of jeans. She buttoned her blouse. "I planned on spending Christmas with my mom and dad. I have a six thirty a.m. flight to LAX on the twenty-sixth. Can you…stay until then?"

Alex zipped up his slacks and pulled a black turtleneck sweater over his head. "I can under one condition… do you have plans for New Year's Eve?" he said as he combed his fingers through his black hair.

She grinned. "Really, Dr. Messina, you're my fake date, what do you think?"

"This may have started as a fake out, but you know there's definitely something between us. I want to see a hell of a lot more of you." He slid his hand under her blouse.

In a tremulous whisper, she said, "More of me now… or in L.A.?"

"Both." He pulled her into him and kissed her.

She patted his cheek and wiggled her brows. "Will you be late for your conference call, or do you have time for coffee and a cinnamon roll before you start working?"

They went down to the kitchen. Kate made a pot of coffee and warmed a cinnamon roll for Alex. "I'm going to take these with me so I can get started on my conference call." He kissed her cheek and left the kitchen.

Alex had said that this Christmas with her was the closest he'd come to a family Christmas in New York since his parents died. He'd missed the kinds of Christmases his mother made for them. He'd said that his mother used to bake gingerbread cookies for him and his sister Caroline. A week before Christmas, they'd put together a gingerbread house. His mother would lay out all the pieces, the candy, and the icing. His reminiscing had given Kate an idea.

She sat at the counter with her coffee when her mother walked into the kitchen. "Hi, Mom. I made coffee."

"Good morning, dear. It smells good."

"I'll get you a cup. What are your plans for today?" she said as she poured a cup of coffee for her mother.

"Olivia has a shopping spree planned for us. She spent the night at her apartment with Ben, so we're meeting them downtown."

"Would you mind if I baked?"

"No, I don't mind."

"Do you still have the cookie cutters for the mini gingerbread house?" Kate asked.

"Yes, in the pantry with all the other molds and cookie cutters; they're all labeled."

Kate checked the pantry and found the ingredients to make gingerbread cookies. Her mom had gone to dress and get ready to go out, so Kate had the kitchen to herself. By mid-morning, the kitchen smelled great. The cookies had cooled, and she'd decorated them. She made a second pot of coffee and hesitated about interrupting Alex. She didn't need to worry because a few minutes later, he walked into the kitchen.

"What are you doing? The wonderful smell of baking is wafting through the house."

He's so handsome. "I made them for you, but I wasn't sure if I should interrupt you. I'm glad you followed the aroma."

He snatched an iced cookie from the cooling rack and bit into it. His eyes closed, and his dark lashes lay against his cheeks. "Mmmm… Kate, it's delicious."

She was so happy to do this small thing for him after all he was doing for her.

"Want coffee?" she said.

"Yes, thanks."

Kate poured two cups of coffee into her mother's Christmas china and removed two plates from the cabinet. She took the special gingerbread man decorated with a red

Santa hat, white icing for the eyes and mouth, and three red dots for his coat.

"Here for you," she said, bringing the plate to the table.

He laughed. "So, you've finally found a Santa hat." He bit into the cookie and then sipped his coffee. "Is this what you've been doing all morning?"

"When you talked about your childhood, I just wanted to do a little something for you."

He leaned over and kissed her. "Thank you, this is a great treat. I had better get back to work. I was almost finished when the smell of the cookies lured me away." He rose from his seat.

"Wait." She went to the counter by the double ovens and brought over the tray where she'd placed the mini gingerbread house sections. On the tray, she'd added some small ramekins with colored gumdrops, pieces of chocolate candy, other mini candy pieces, along with the bag of thick white icing.

"Do you have time to build this house?" She lifted her brows and couldn't control her grin from spreading into a smile.

"You did this for me?" His gaze held a glint of wonder.

She nodded back at him, her pulse racing. "After all you're doing for me, this is the least I could do." *Fake dating, making real love to me, and not just sex.*

His knuckle caressed her cheek. "Will you help me build it?"

"I baked it. Now I have to build it?" She grumped at him.

"It's better together." He put his arms around her waist and hugged her to him. "Where is everyone?"

"They went to town for last-minute Christmas shopping. They'll be gone for hours." Her arms looped around his neck.

Alex looked down at her, his emerald-green eyes twinkling below the fringe of his dark lashes as he pulled her into his strong arms. One powerful hand pressed the curve of her buttocks into him.

"You smell like gingerbread… let's see if you taste like that." Alex's hand slid up her cheek, his fingers sliding along her neck.

Desire hot and wild filled her, and she opened her lips to him.

His mouth covered hers. Kate melted against his rippling muscles, pressing her breasts against his sweater-clad chest. Alex slipped his tongue into her waiting mouth, rubbing his tongue on hers.

"Mmmm." He lifted his mouth from hers. "Gingerbread and coffee."

"My family won't be home for several hours…"

"What do you have in mind?" He didn't give her a chance to answer. "Never mind. I have an idea." He scooped Kate into his powerful arms and headed for the stairs. Taking the stairs two at a time up to her bedroom.

"I knew you'd think of something," she said, running her tongue along his ear.

"Keep doing that, and we won't make it to the bed," he said, standing her on her feet just inside her room. He closed and locked the door.

THEY'D JUST SPENT an hour in her room, making love. "What's on the agenda for this afternoon?" Alex said as he came out of the en suite.

"I guess after lunch and shopping, they're going to decorate the living room Christmas tree. I don't know why they've waited so long. My parents usually buy a tree and decorate it by December fifteenth at the latest."

Alex stepped into his pants and zipped them. "I had better

go back to your dad's office and finish up. Then I can give you moral support. I'm guessing Dan and Brittany will be here as well?"

I love the way he's looking out for me. "Yes, of course. Bridezilla wants this to be a family affair." Kate smoothed the comforter back over the bed.

Alex kissed her before he left the room.

～

KATE WALKED into the living room dreading tree decorating but was willing to make the best of it. Olivia sat on the floor, opening some of the boxes with Christmas ornaments. The garland lay in a neat pile next to her and the clear lights in a neat circle, ready to be strung on the tree.

"Hi, where is everybody?" Kate asked.

Her sister didn't look up and continued with what she was doing as she said, "Mom and Dad are upstairs. Ben is getting the bows from the attic, and Dan and Brittany will be here soon."

"Yippee, the whole family together again," Kate snarked.

Ben walked into the living room with his arms full of boxes. "Hello, Kate, ready for the fun?"

Olivia jumped up from the floor, putting her hands on her hips. She didn't give Kate a chance to answer Ben before she said, "Why can't you be friends for my sake? Dan and Brittany have moved on and are happy together. They're so excited for the baby's arrival," Olivia said, picking up the lights.

Yes, exactly what I wanted, a family. She took that from me too.
"She—" Olivia began.

Kate had had enough. "I can't talk to you," she said before storming from the room. Her sister could be so mean at times. She wasn't clueless; no, she was inconsiderate. Kate ran up the stairs and down the hall to her room. She held her tears until she opened her bedroom door. She let out a shriek of anger, then swiped at her eyes. She closed the door and stopped short. "I thought you were in my dad's office working."

She turned, trying to hide her face and the tears that streamed down her cheeks.

"I finished." Alex came over to her, his hands resting on her shoulders, sliding to her upper arms as he held her. She bent her head and leaned her back into Alex's chest.

"Tell me why you're crying." His lips brushed her ear as he spoke.

She sniffed. "Was there ever anyone special? The one you wanted to spend the rest of your life with."

His fingers curled on her shoulders, his thumbs massaging the tension from her back. "A couple of years ago… It didn't work out."

"Why?"

He turned her in his arms. "Kate, what's this all about. Why the tears?"

She moved her head and hid her face against his chest, hating the way her crying thickened her voice. "My sister thinks that Dan, Britany, and I should be friends because of her. Why should I be friends with them? He broke my heart, and Brittany didn't care that he had a wife. I can't be friends with them, I won't. She's having the baby *I* wanted. Olivia is lucky I agreed to be her maid of honor while Dan is best man. It turns my stomach each time I think of how he betrayed my trust. While I was killing myself working, he was hooking up with her."

"You have every right to feel this way. Didn't you tell Olivia how you feel?"

"She told me I was selfish and only thinking of myself."

"You, selfish? Impossible. I will say that this is awkward

and something you'll have to come to terms with for your sake and your parents. It must be hurting them as well."

Wow, he really is compassionate. "They're the reason I came home… Dr. Messina, are you also a psychiatrist? Can you prescribe some therapy for me?" She wiped the tears from her face, and Alex reached into his back pocket and handed her his handkerchief.

He tucked a loose curl behind her ear. "Do you know how beautiful you are? You drive me crazy."

"You're good for my ego." She reached out, touching his cheek.

He wrapped his arms around her waist and tugged her against his body. "Let me show you over and over what else I'm good for."

His lips brushed hers. She reached up and kissed him. Her hands skimmed over his arms, his biceps. She leaned into his strong, broad chest, and her arms went around his waist.

Alex ran his fingers through her hair, turning her face to his. His thumbs wiped at her tears. "I only want your happiness."

"Alex," she groaned. *I can't be lied to again.*

"Wait here. I'll be right back." He went into the en suite and returned with a washcloth.

"Here, let me."

"I must look terrible." She tried to hide her face.

"Not to me, Kate. You're beautiful." He pressed the cold towel to her eyes. Then he tossed the towel onto the hamper.

"Come here," he said, wrapping her into his arms. He kissed her temple before the tip of his finger circled her left breast through the silk fabric of her blouse.

"I felt a connection that I've never had with anyone else. I know you felt it too. I want to give you a commitment."

"Just like that? You don't know me. We met three days ago."

"I know everything I need to know." His emerald-green eyes impaled her. His sculpted lips slowly lowering to hers brushing her lips, slowly increasing the pressure of his lips over hers. He cupped her buttocks in his big hands and lifted her. She wrapped her legs around his waist. Kate felt as if their souls touched. "Do you need to know anything else?" he said against her lips.

"No, you're right. Don't ever stop...kissing me." He spun around with her in his arms. Kate laughed as he fell back onto her bed with her coming down on top of him. "Oh, Alex, you're the best. I'm so happy we met on the plane."

He slipped his fingers into her hair, pushing a curl behind her ear. "Me too, beautiful. How about we get dressed? I made reservations at an Italian restaurant in the village. I know the owners. They're from Naples... very authentic food."

"I like Italian food." Kate rolled off Alex and went to open her closet door. She stood for a moment, deciding what to wear. *Yes*, she reached for the lace cocktail dress she'd planned on wearing to her sister's Christmas Eve engagement party.

There was a knock on her bedroom door. "Ugh, I hope it's not Olivia. I don't want to deal with her now," Kate whispered over her shoulder to Alex.

"I'll take care of it." He got up from the bed, walked to the door, and opened it. "Ben," he said.

"Hi, can I talk to Kate for a moment?" he said.

"Come in," Kate said. She always liked Dan's kid brother. He ran his hand through his dark, curly hair as he walked into the bedroom.

Alex stood next to Kate, his emerald-green gaze searching her eyes. Kate gave the slightest nod. "I'm going to get dressed in the en suite, so you and Ben can have some privacy here." He kissed her brow and gave her a squeeze before he turned to go.

Ben sat in the accent chair by the bed, while she sat at the foot of her bed. "Kate, I'm sorry. Your sister can be dense at times. This situation is so messed up. I don't know what happened between you, Dan, and Brittany, but I am truly sorry. I know they must have hurt you terribly. I asked Olivia not to force a friendship that can't be... I'm so relieved that Dan and Brittany hadn't arrived when she started nagging you."

"Ben, I know she can be immature at times, and you are definitely good for her. I see how much you love her, and I'm happy for you both. I wouldn't have agreed to be maid of honor if I didn't care for you too."

Kate stood and walked to Ben and hugged him before kissing him on his cheek. "Thanks." She patted his cheek. "By the way, I like your five o'clock shadow beard."

He gave her a hug. "Kate, I'm happy we're going to be related again."

While she and Ben spoke, Alex had dressed in his navy-blue suit, an ice-blue silk shirt, and his blue-and-grey-striped tie. After Ben left, Kate said, "Very handsome, Dr. Messina." She brushed imaginary lint from his lapel. Then she hurried to get dressed. She applied eyeliner and a coral glossy tint to her lips.

"You're stunning in that dress." He reached for her hand, turned it palm up, and placed a kiss in the center.

They walked down the stairs holding hands and strolled into the living room. The rest of the group was already there having drinks.

When Brittany saw Kate, she slid closer to Dan and whispered to him. He nodded and went to the bar. He returned with a glass of sparkling water for her.

"Hello, all," Alex said to the group sitting in the living room.

"The tree looks really great, Mom. You did a good job," Kate said, pleased at how composed she sounded.

The majestic balsam fir looked as if it belonged in Santa's village and not in front of the large bow window. The live tree was decorated with red and green velvet bows, white lights, and gold rope garland.

Kate's mom and dad sat on the sofa near the tree, and Olivia and Ben stood by the large window, while Dan and Brittany sat on the love seat. She sipped her water before placing the glass on a coaster on the coffee table. It was a cozy group and if it weren't for her ex-husband and his new wife, Kate would have liked to join them before they left for dinner.

Kate did her best to ignore Dan and Brittany.

Olivia said, "I guess you ordered a limousine. One just pulled up out front." She peered out, her nose almost touching the window. "Oh, it's a Rolls Royce."

"Yes, we're going to dinner first. Alex picked an Italian restaurant in the Village, then the show." She kissed her mom and dad before they left.

They took their coats from the hall closet on the way out to the limo. Kate slid onto the soft leather of the backseat of the Rolls Royce, and Alex followed. The driver closed their door, and Alex pressed a button on the console. Kate watched as the privacy partition went from opaque to solid for total privacy.

She compressed her lips into a thin line and shook her head.

Alex gazed at her. "Why the frown?"

Kate huffed. "Do you see what Brittany does when I'm around?"

"You mean hold onto Dan for dear life?" He chuckled.

"Yes, what does she think, I'm going to steal him back from her? Good riddance to him. She deserves the cheater."

"I know it's a sore subject for you, but do you know how Dan met Brittany?"

Kate blew out her breath. "Oh, I know, all right. I introduced them."

Alex's head snapped toward her, his eyes wide. "What?"

"Yes, she worked at the law firm where I work. She was a front desk receptionist while going to college for her bachelor's degree. She wanted to go to law school, and she asked me about the entrance exam. I offered to help her and occasionally, we'd go out to lunch. One day... Dan came to take me to lunch, and as they say, the rest is history."

"I'm sorry, Kate," Alex slid his arm around her shoulder. "Now you have me, and you're the only woman I'll ever want."

He pressed a button on the console, and the side windows turned to black, and the interior roof lit with pinpoints of light, like stars in a night sky. *Wow, my first ride in a Rolls, and he seems so comfortable.*

He slid his arm down to hold her hand, entwining their fingers. Then he brushed his thumb over her wrist. "I'm your plus one for life, Kate Thompson, and I want more than dating... I want a commitment."

"Alex, I... want that too." *You better not hurt me.*

"Let's toast with champagne," he said, pressing a button on the side door console. A cooler compartment popped open to reveal a champagne bottle and two flutes. He popped the cork and poured the liquid, it bubbled and fizzed. Then he handed her a glass.

"Here's to us, Kate. I never thought I'd meet my destiny on a flight from L.A. to New York."

"I'm glad we met." They touched glasses and sipped the champagne. He bent toward her and kissed her moist lips.

"We'll have a funny story to tell our kids." He snuggled her closer to his side.

"Kids? I'm—"

His lips ran along her neck, and his husky voice sent shivers up her spine. "Yes, lots of them. Little girls who look just like you."

He remembered what I said about Brittany having the family I wanted. Can I trust him with my heart?

Alex said, "We have to tell your parents the truth about us. It's not fair to them."

"I know my dad really likes you, but sooner or later, I'll have to be the one to tell them. It's my responsibility since I allowed this."

"It's no longer a lie though, so I think it will work out. I would like to be with you when you tell them."

"After the engagement party... Christmas Day. It will only be the four of us, so maybe that would be a good time... I could say—Merry Christmas—Mom and Dad, we lied to you."

"You're an attorney. I'm confident that you'll find a way to be diplomatic."

Kate laughed, feeling happy for the first time since she found out her sister was engaged to Ben.

CHAPTER 8

The morning of the engagement party, the weather had turned bitterly cold, dropping to the mid-twenties. The forecast said no snow, and that was great since some of the guests were flying in from Florida, and others were driving to Long Island from the city and surrounding areas.

Kate walked into the toasty warm family room. Her mother sat in a wing chair by the fireplace with her hands wrapped around a snowman mug.

"Hello, dear. I made hot chocolate. Would you like some?"

"No, thanks. Mom, do you need me to come with you to the reception hall? Maybe lend a hand with any last-minute items? I know I haven't been much help."

Her mother beamed. "Everything is taken care of for tonight. I met with the event coordinator yesterday, and the tables were already set up." She leaned forward in her seat, her eyes full of excitement. "Wait until you see the cute decorations and the centerpieces."

"What kind—

"No. I want you to be surprised."

Her mom's excitement was contagious, and Kate laughed. "Okay, but Olivia is the one who needs to be surprised. After all, it's her party." Kate tucked her feet under her on the green wing chair.

Her mom continued, "I can share this. The baker has made a beautiful cake, and we ordered iced cookies with Ben and Olivia's names, some in the shape of engagement rings and other cute cutouts. We kept the Christmas colors for all the decorations."

"I know how much you love to do these kinds of fun things." Kate laughed. "Remember when you were our Girl Scout leader, we always had the best parties."

"Yes, I do love to plan parties. I controlled my enthusiasm and made Olivia help. She chose all the couples' activities."

That figures. Kate nodded but didn't say anything.

Her mom said, "Later, we're going to do hair and makeup."

"Mom, I'm... not sure... about that if—"

"It's only going to be the three of us, no one else. Remember, like when you were younger, and we'd have girls night? Just me and my two girls. No one else is invited."

"Then yes." Kate pulled her hair up and twisted it on top of her head. "What do you think? Something like this?" She stretched her neck, tilting her head from side to side.

Her mom laughed and clapped her hands in excitement. "Definitely an updo will be perfect for tonight."

"What time are we meeting for hair and makeup?"

"I thought around four this afternoon will give us plenty of time."

"Well then, I guess I'll go find Alex."

"Dad and Alex went out," her mom said. She put her finger to her lips and looked around the room. Then she said in a whisper, "I guess Alex needs a present for someone."

Kate sat up in the chair. *I completely forgot about Christmas*

Day when Alex and I would spend the time with my parents. We never discussed presents. She jumped up from her seat. "I need to run to the store. Can I borrow the car?"

"Yes, of course, dear. Didn't you two plan on exchanging gifts?"

"Ah... yes... for sure... we did. I just didn't have time. Mom, I really need to get going."

"Okay, feel free to take the car."

"Thanks, Mom," Kate said and hurried from the room. *What to get him? Ugh, Christmas Eve Day at the mall, will I find a parking space?*

Kate remembered the local jeweler in their town. He had some of the most unique and best jewelry items, including jewelry from high-end designers.

Traffic on the two-lane road into town wasn't too bad. She parked her mother's BMW on the street near the jewelry store. She hurried to the store and browsed the window before she was buzzed into the store. Once in, she walked to the men's section and peered into the Christmas-decorated glass showcases. Men's wristwatches were on display in the first showcase. *No, he's been wearing a nice Rolex.* She moved down to the next showcase. Cufflinks, tie clips, tie pins, tuxedo shirt studs. Kate remembered that most his of shirts had French cuffs. *You could never have too many cufflinks.* She found the perfect gift for Alex. Double G Gucci cufflinks in sterling silver.

Driving back to her parents' home, she was pleased with her gift. She couldn't wait for Christmas morning to give them to him. When she arrived back home, she went right up to her room to hide her present. She pulled down her secret hiding place, an old shoebox on the top shelf of her closet, and placed the present in it.

Kate grabbed her cosmetic travel bag and went up to her

parents' bedroom. It was time to get ready for the party. "Hi, I'm ready to play dress up."

Olivia giggled. "You're late. I've started." She sat at the hair dressing station her mom had set up, complete with various sizes of curling irons, hair clips, and styling products.

Her mom said, "Come join the fun. I have a tray with sandwiches, another with cookies… and… spiked hot chocolate in the thermal carafe."

"Yes, hot chocolate and a cookie for me," she said as she walked over to pour a cup. "Anyone else want something?"

"No, thanks," Olivia and her mom said at the same time.

"I see the makeup station is all set up." Kate sipped her drink and went to sit in front of the mirror. "I brought my own makeup. Olivia, can you help me do a smokey dramatic look?"

"Sure, once Mom finishes with my hair."

"This is so much fun. I remember when you were kids, and you'd both sneak up here to play with my makeup."

"Mom, I'll never forget your face when you found Olivia hadn't only covered her face in red lipstick, but she managed to get lipstick on the tub, the sink, and the carpet by your bed."

"What was I, three?" Olivia laughed.

"The worst was having to explain dress up to your father, and that we needed to replace the entire bedroom carpet."

They finished curling each other's hair and helped apply makeup. Kate had fun with her mom and sister. The three of them laughed and joked like kids.

Kate rushed back to her room. She took her beautiful red dress off the hanger. Slipping out of her robe, she hurried to get the dress on, hiding her sexy lingerie before Alex could see. *Tonight, I'll be happy to let him strip these off me.*

Alex walked out of the en suite, his long fingers giving a

final adjustment to his bow tie. "Do you need help with the zipper?"

"OMG, you look beyond handsome in your tux. Have I told you I'm a pushover for a man in a tux?"

He wiggled his brows at her. "That's definitely good to know. Let me get that zipper for you."

Kate stood in front of the full-length mirror in her bedroom.

Alex stood behind her, his spicy scent filling her head. He slid the side zipper of her gown up her body while he spread kisses along her neck and shoulder. "I've been wanting to do that ever since you tried this on at Saks," he whispered against her skin.

Her body rippled with excitement as she gazed at him in the mirror. "Later… I'm hoping you help me out of the dress as well," she said in a broken whisper.

He nipped her neck. "Yes, definitely." His big hands slid around her waist, dragging her back against his hard body. "Then I'm going to make you come so many times, you won't remember where you are."

Kate grinned, vigorously nodding her head. *Do we have to go to this stupid party?*

"Are you two ready? The limo is here," her mother said from the stairs, startling Kate.

"Yes, Mom. We're on our way." Kate tried to keep the frustration from her voice.

Alex handed Kate her gold beaded evening bag, and they went down the stairs to the living room. Kate's mom stood near the entry in a beautiful electric-blue, beaded ball gown, a velvet cloak draped over her arm. Her black hair tucked behind her ears to show her sparkly chandelier earrings. Kate's dad sat on the sofa in his tuxedo.

Ben waited for Olivia to come down the stairs. She looked beautiful in an iridescent, pleated, bare-shouldered ball gown. Earlier, Ben had surprised her with a diamond necklace which now encircled her slim neck. Her strawberry-blond long hair was tied away from her face, and tiny ringlets bounced and moved as she walked.

When they arrived at the reception hall, they heard piano music from outside. "I'm so excited," Olivia said to them. "Mom wouldn't let me see the room once it was decorated."

"I'm sure you're going to love everything," Kate said.

A Christmas tree decorated with gold ornaments stood to one side of the room. Christmas wreaths hung from the Palladian windows across the back of the room. Lanterns lit the patio and although it was too cold to go out, it was very pretty. Eight round tables covered in white damask tablecloths surrounded by ten chairs with red bows hanging from the gold spindle backs. One smaller table stood out from the rest with only two chairs for Olivia and Ben.

"Let's find where we're sitting," Kate said.

Alex put his hand on the small of her back, and they walked over to the table with all of the place cards. "Here we are. Table one," she said, reaching for the card. Before they reached the table, her cousin Jane put her hands to her cheeks and said, "Oh my God, look at you! You're gorgeous."

Kate laughed at her cousin. "Alex, this is my cousin Jane. You'll have to excuse her."

"But he *is* gorgeous." They laughed as her aunt and uncle joined them. She kissed them and introduced Alex to her relatives.

Kate and Alex sat and chatted with Jane, while the rest of the guests from their table were on the dance floor. Dan and Brittany walked past their table. Jane sneered at them, then turned to Alex and said, "My cousin is so much better off without that POS. It was Kate's lucky day when she came home from work at lunchtime to find the dirty bastard in bed with that bitch."

Kate gasped, and her eyebrows lifted. "Jane."

She leaned back in her chair. "It's okay, cuz."

"Alex, I—"

Alex took Kate's hand and brought it to his lips. "Let's dance." Holding her hand, he led her onto the parquet dance floor and wrapped his arms around her. "I hope Jane doesn't think I'm rude leaving her alone at the table. This is the only way I can hug you here."

"I'm sorry. My cousin shouldn't have said what she did."

He held her in his arms, swaying to the music. "What do you mean? They were terrible to you?" He kissed her temple. "You have me now. I'm your forever plus one."

Kate wrapped her arms around his neck. The scent of his cologne enticed her, and she rested her head on his shoulder. "Mmmm."

IT WAS after midnight and now officially Christmas Day when the limousine dropped Kate, Alex, and her parents at home. Olivia and Ben were going to their apartment. The next day, they would spend Christmas with his parents.

"Mom, you did a great job. The party was a huge success." Kate kissed her cheek, then she and Alex said good night to her parents and went up to her bedroom.

Alex opened the dresser drawer where his shirts and sweaters were neatly folded and removed a gift box. "Merry Christmas," he said.

Kate went to the closet and came back to Alex with her gift for him. "Merry Christmas."

He sat on the bed. "You go first."

"Okay." Kate recognized the red-and-gold Cartier box. When she opened the lid, warmth radiated through her body.

The gold-and-diamond love bangle gleamed. "Oh, Alex, it's beautiful."

"I had it inscribed."

Kate lifted the bangle from its velvet cradle and read the inscription. *December 20. Your forever plus one.* "The day we met." Kate lay the box on the bed and wrapped her arms around his neck. She brushed her lips on his velvety smooth ones. "Merry Christmas."

Alex pulled her across his lap, taking the pins from her hair and running his fingers through the length.

"Wait, open your gift." Kate's excitement bubbled in her voice. "I hope you like it."

He unwrapped the outer box of the present and opened the lid. Alex kissed her temple. "Thank you, I'll wear them tomorrow." She looped her arms around his neck.

"Kate, we're not going to steal anyone's thunder, but when we get home to L.A., I want you to come with me to pick out an engagement ring. I don't want to wait; we're old enough to know what we've found in each other."

She melted into his arms. "Yes, we can go to Las Vegas and get married." She spread kisses over his face.

"Right now, I want to deliver on my earlier promise. I'm going to make you come so many times, you won't remember where you are." He fell back on the bed, taking her with him. She felt the rough heat of his hand slide up her legs.

"Mmmm, we have to get you out of this dress." His husky voice breathed against her neck.

"Yes, yes, hurry."

His fingers were at her zipper, and she pulled at his bow tie. She stood long enough for her gown to slither to the floor. He threw his jacket off and eased his fly down. She throbbed and with shaking fingers, she tore his shirt open. Studs flew in all directions. Her eyes fluttered shut. They were naked. She was wet and ready. He held her waist and lifted her onto his huge erection.

"Ahhh, yes." She straddled him, lifting and lowering herself onto his steel-hard shaft. It didn't take too long for the coil in her belly to release into a mindless orgasm.

He held her hips down as he pumped up into her. Her body shuddered, her head tilted back as she rode him to another wild orgasm. He held her in his arms and slid up to rest against the headboard. Kissing her breasts, sucking on the nipples. Kate held his head to her breasts as pleasure tore into her. "Oh God, yes, yes. Again." Her body writhed against him in multiple orgasms.

He nipped at her neck. "More, Kate?"

"Yes, yes, but you too." She pulled him over to lie on top of her. He kissed her.

"I'll be right back," he said. They were up most of the night.

Alex cuddled against her back. His knees were tucked under her, their fingers entwined. "What was Christmas breakfast like when you were young?"

"After Caroline and I tore into all the presents, my mother would make french toast for us. She would use Panettone, an Italian Christmas bread filled with dried fruit. She would make thick slices of that served with breakfast sausages or ham. My father would make Bellinis for us, naturally virgin for Caroline and me."

"That sounds so good. One day, I'll make that for you. Right now, I smell coffee."

"I'm going to shave and get dressed. Then we can go have breakfast with your parents."

Kate sat up in bed and looked around the room. *What a mess we made.* She slipped into her red satin robe, tying the belt around her waist. She found her gown in a pool on the floor, exactly where Alex had stripped it from her. His tuxedo jacket was on the floor, and his pants were thrown into a corner. His shirt was on the floor under the chair, along with her bra and panties. She found her garter and stockings by the nightstand. As she bent to pick them up from the floor, a flash caught her eye. *Alex's phone must have slid under the bed last night.*

Kate put his phone on the nightstand by the bed. She hung her dress and smoothed his pants over her arm. On her way to find a hanger for his tux, his phone vibrated with a text. Kate tried not to look at his phone, but then she couldn't help it.

Hi handsome, filming will go on into mid-January. I miss you so, so much and can't wait to have our own special Christmas. Merry Christmas, love ya, Carlotta.

At the end of the text were two hearts.

KATE FROZE. Everything stopped—breathing, thinking, her heart. *He lied to me.* He was seeing someone, and he just had some free time. Oh, the dirty bastard, telling me we would get married. They were all the same, every single last one of them—liars and cheaters.

Why? There is no one to turn to or talk with—not like the last time when I stayed with Jane—She had to get through today. First thing tomorrow morning, she'd catch her flight home. He was a lying, no good SOB just in nice Armani suits and now Gucci cufflinks. *What a fool I am to believe him. I didn't learn my lessons very well after Dan and Brittany, now did I?*

When Alex walked into the bedroom, she was ready. "You lied to me." She pointed to the phone on the nightstand. "Liar," she hissed at him.

"What are you talking about?" His brows came together.

"A text from Carlotta, that's what." Her voice rose with her anger.

His nostrils flared, and he stood with his feet apart. "You read my text? You don't know who she is?"

"I know what I read," she snapped.

"Really? You always jump to conclusions. How could you possibly know?" He thundered and jabbed a finger to his chest. "I don't want to be clumped into your cheaters category. I poured my heart out to you, and you can't ask me who she is."

"There aren't may famous people who go by one name," Kate shouted. "Cher, Madonna, *and* Carlotta. She's the most beautiful woman in the world, and you're seeing her." Kate heard the bitterness in her voice. "She can't wait to celebrate a special Christmas with you when filming is over."

She sniffed. "I didn't mean to read the entire text, but once I started, I couldn't stop. Now I'm happy I did. You just wanted someone to pass the time with. What a fool I am to believe you loved me and wanted to marry me."

His voice hardened. "You have no idea what you're saying. Aren't you a criminal trial attorney? Don't you investigate the facts, or do you jump to conclusions at work as well? I wouldn't want you to represent me—not even for a traffic ticket—Kate Thompson."

Kate threw open her bedroom door. "I don't want you to stay here today. I want you to get out now. You miserable liar. Did you work on Carlotta? Is that how you met? Her beauty had to come through your surgical skills."

He stormed to the closet and yanked his suitcase from the shelf. He slammed it onto her bed. "Believe me, you have no idea what you're saying." He threw his shirts into his bag. "You don't have to tell me twice. I'm getting out of here today —Now." His voice thundered through her.

Her parents stood at the open bedroom door, her mother's eyes wide and her father shaking his head. "What is all this yelling? Kate, you never raise your voice. What's going on?" her dad said.

"He's not my boyfriend. I met him on the plane ride here, and this is all fake. Fake dating, fake relationship, fake, fake, fake."

Alex stopped packing, folded his arms across his chest, and smirked. "That was diplomatic," he snickered.

Too late, Kate realized what she had blurted out, covered her mouth, and shook her head.

"You may think this is fake," her mom said, "but the way you two act and look into each other's eyes when you think no one is around. There's definitely love between you and Alex."

Her dad, with his brows furrowed, turned to Alex. "Is it true you met Kate on the plane and cooked up this story? Are... you really a doctor?"

"Yes, sir. I am really who I say I am, Alexander Messina M.D., and I love your daughter. Although, at this moment—"

"Ha, ha," Kate snarked. "How could he when he's going to spend a *special* belated Christmas with Carlotta?" She gritted her teeth.

Alex turned to Kate, his fingers curling into fists planted on his hips. He bent so that they were eye level, almost nose to nose, before he ground the words out between his teeth. "Do you want to know who Carlotta is?"

She sniffed. "I know who she is. The most beautiful woman in the world, and you're dating her."

Alex's gaze held hers, his eyes, flashing green fire. "Carlotta... is Caroline... my sister."

The only sound in the room was Kate's gasp before her mouth fell open. *Sister?* "Sister! You couldn't tell me that sooner?"

"Why, Kate?" His voice was heavy with sarcasm. "You wanted me to save you from jumping to conclusions."

Her father stepped into the room. "Why don't you two take a breather and come down to breakfast?"

"Alex is leaving," Kate mumbled.

Isla laughed. "Have you looked out the window? Neither of you can go anywhere today. It snowed in the night. Not too much, but enough that flights at JFK have been cancelled." Kate hurried to the window and pulled the drapes open.

"Great."

"Plenty of time for you two to discuss your situation. I have coffee ready for you," Isla said and tugged on Bill's sleeve. "Let's go down to the kitchen."

Kate and Alex stared at each other. They couldn't miss the giggles from her parents. Her father laughed before he said loud enough for her and Alex to hear, "Fake dating. Isla, have you ever? It looked pretty real to me. The way Alex shielded her from Dan. I didn't see anything fake from either of those two."

"We can hear you, you know," Kate said.

"Shhhh, shhh, we better leave them alone," her mom said between giggles.

Kate shook her head and muttered, "They're worse than teenagers."

She raised her gaze to Alex. His arms were once more crossed over his broad chest. "Alex, you must believe me." She hung her head before she gazed into his emerald-green eyes. "I've never acted so badly in all my life. And yes… I have to stop jumping to conclusions." Kate took a ragged breath. "Dan and Brittany did a number on me. My personal life is a disaster, but that's no excuse. I do trust you. I'm so very sorry that I didn't give you a chance to explain. I just assumed." She bit her lip. "I'm sorry."

Alex dropped his arms and took a step closer to Kate. "I know what you've been through. I would never cause you pain. I love you."

Her head snapped up as a smile spread across her lips. "I think I've always known that. I love you, Alex Messina."

He pulled her into his embrace and kissed her forehead. "I think once the airport opens, we should fly straight to Las Vegas and get married."

"Yes, that's a great idea." Kate rose on her toes and looped her arms around his neck. "You know, you had me at Santa hat," she whispered in his ear.

THANK you for reading *A Fake Date for Kate*. I hope you enjoyed Kate and Alex's love story.

Read Carlotta's story in *The Christmas Present*. It's the short love story of Caroline and Brandon.

She hates him, but tell that to her traitorous body. Grab your copy here.

The Christmas Present
Sign up for my newsletter and receive a free download of
THE CHRISTMAS PRESENT
https://dl.bookfunnel.com/cuazfkmzsz

www.CindyReddingAuthor.com

ALSO BY CINDY REDDING

The DiMarco Empire
The Sicilian's Betrayal
The Winemaker's Seduction
The Frenchman's Revenge
The Sea Captain's Redemption

Christmas
A Fake Date for Kate

The Royals
A Royal Temptation

More Romances
The Tycoon's Secret Child

www.CindyReddingAuthor.com

WHERE TO FIND MY BOOKS

You can find my books at your favorite bookstore, retailer, or library

Or, you can buy them directly from me at my website https:// CindyReddingAuthor.com

Or,

Cindy's Store https://payhip.com/CindyRedding

If you prefer, please scan this QR Code with your phone

ABOUT THE AUTHOR

USA TODAY Bestselling Author **Cindy Redding** fell in love with happily ever after when she read her first romance at age twelve. Since then, she has been hooked.

A native New Yorker, Cindy lived on the beach in South Florida and now she lives in Las Vegas, NV, with her husband, of thirty-five years whom she married on Valentine's Day. She has two daughters. Her eldest is named after a heroine in one of Cindy's favorite romances.

Inspired by her travels around the world and her love of Italy Cindy's, sizzling contemporary romance novels come to life with hot men and the strong-willed, independent women who they can't live without.

Escape into a world were happily ever after, lives.

www.ingramcontent.com/pod-product-compliance
Lightning Source LLC
Chambersburg PA
CBHW051712180726
48283CB00004B/1317